The Dog Who Came For Christmas

Christmas

Jody Sharpe

If There Are No Dogs in Heaven, Then When I Die, I Want to Go Where They
Went

Will Rogers (1879-1935)

For Maggie

Prologue

I fly this Christmas night over the sleepy town of Mystic Bay, California. Most of the people in the world below are tucked into to bed. The stills of the winter night always take my breath away. The townsfolk here say they live in a tiny slice of heaven. Yet, little do they know that there are angels here like me living a human existence. We agree that Mystic Bay is near and dear to heaven for it was here a few years back that angels appeared to children with special needs. Since then, nothing has been the same.

It's a well- kept secret that I am Angel Ken, an earth living angel. My owl companion, leads the way as I peer down at lone midnight walker, Jamie Bond, and his dogs, Bondo and Riley. Dogs and all animals see us angels flying by. Jamie waves while still looking straight ahead, knowing an angel is flying above them. Jamie hasn't seen an angel yet but believes they are near and that his faithful dogs surely see us. I fly over Gayle and Alex Knight's house, spotting them below on their patio, looking at the night. It was the beginning of December that their Christmas story unfolded. It's a story that needs to be told. It is one where intuition and love's triumph changed lives, both furry and human. But this is not a story for me, an angel, to tell. Little miracles happen every day in Mystic Bay and this little miracle story is one of my favorites.

The Dog Who Came for Christmas.

Chapter 1

December 1st - Another Dream

I t's 4 am and I'm awake about to get out of bed to prepare for my job as the weekend meteorologist at KHBW TV in San Francisco. My name is Gayle Force Knight, a slightly psychic townsperson of Mystic Bay. I have to say that my dream last night was another prophetic one. The angel, who I always see in my dreams, was holding my dear departed childhood dog, Dukie. In the dream, swirled into a vision was me meeting a dog today at Bay Star Shelter in downtown San Francisco. I will be interviewing the director there and a philanthropist I know who is helping promote a Christmas fundraiser while also publicizing his renovation of empty buildings for apartment living for the homeless population. In the dream's vision, I will meet a black dog with a white muzzle and patches. She will run to me and I will take her home. Then the vision becomes a scene where the dog and I will be embarking on a journey to rescue another dog like dear Dukie. But wait! Did I see neighbor, Ken Leighton there too? Will he help me rescue even more dogs? I don't know Ken well but I do know he is really an angel living a human life in our beloved town.

As the angel and Dukie disappeared, the angel whispered, "*Christmas miracles coming your way.*" The dream vanishes in the morning sky. I rub my eyes, ready for the day but with trepidation. Last time I had a prophetic dream, my husband, Alex and I solved a would-be crime. But is this dream about another crime about to happen?

I get up as our two dogs, Magic and Ralph, sleep soundly in their beds, and our comical cat, Maurice, is wrapped around the smallest one, Magic. As my husband, Alex, groggy from sleep wakes, he says, "Are you okay, honey?"

"Another angel dream, dear. Go back to sleep. I'll tell you about it later."

"Good luck today," he says dreamily.

Quietly, I get ready for my job at KBHW. I reflect on the dream full of adventure with a black and white dog I'm yet to meet. I think about how I always will miss Dukie, the first dog I loved. In my last prophetic dream, my Dream Angel showed me a future crime I had to solve. But this dream is so different. A dog Dukie wants me to meet and another to find? But the best part was that angel had Dukie in her arms.

I shower, dress in my favorite orange pant suit, sweep my hair in the usual ponytail, don the heavy make-up for TV and pour coffee for the ride to the station. Magic and Ralph come trailing behind me but, as I walk out of the room, I see that Maurice has jumped up to be cozy cuddly next to Alex. I take the dogs out back before leaving knowing Alex will feed them when he wakes up. I write him a note and leave it on the counter, telling him the basics of the dream, the angel with Dukie, and of meeting a dog today. I finish with, "Another adventure to go on." I don't elaborate, but offer hope his foot feels better. Poor guy is in a boot from our ski trip last weekend. Ruffling Magic and Ralph's furry heads, I say goodbye, telling Magic maybe next weekend, I will take her with me again to be my Sunday Weather Dog companion. I set off now, taking a deep breath of the salty Pacific air. Dawn is yet to come; the vast ocean is only two blocks from our home. Looking up as I drive out of Mystic Bay, the beauty of the new day inspires me to whisper, "Good morning, magical Mystic Bay." Alex will be working hard today and I'll be excited to tell him everything if I really do meet a black and white dog and find an angel-Dukie mission I need to go on. The mornings lightly clouded moon soothes my soul as fog drifts in to hide the stars. As I drive on, the quiet ride takes me away from my quaint seaside town, on to the foggy lights beyond, to my favorite city by the Bay.

Chapter 2

A Winter Morning

Wrapping up my 7 am weather report, I smile towards the camera, "Well, Bay Area, get ready for a crisp day and on into the night too. Temps about the speed limit, fifty-five degrees. So, bundle up everyone! Enjoy your Sunday, but get that second cup of coffee or tea in your hands to warm you up before you go about. The sun will be shining after the fog lifts. Have a great rest of the weekend! Tomorrow, sixties; finally, a warm-up!"

Chase, our anchor, smiles at me, "Thanks Gayle. Before we say goodbye, tell us about your Christmas piece that will air this week for Good News Around the Bay."

"Yes Chase, I'll be interviewing the director and volunteers at Bay Star Shelter. The shelter is teaming up with Sommerset House and will start its annual Christmas campaign today called, A Christmas of Hope. Donations of money and gifts are needed to help all the children and families at Bay Star Shelter and other outreaches in the Bay Area. I'm honored to be this year's spokesperson. I'll be reporting from Bay Star Shelter and Sommerset House each weekend morning this month. Christmas, I'll be reporting all day for the Christmas meals at the shelter with breakfast, lunch, Santa, and gifts for the children too! Sommerset House is the housing development for individuals and families in need and it's helping fund new apartment housing around the Bay for the homeless population."

"That's really wonderful, Gayle." He turns back to the camera. "Gayle will keep us all posted." As Chase and Mitzy Blane, the new traffic reporter, and I sign off our Sunday morning show, I keep worrying about the meeting today at Bay Star Shelter. I have a psychic feeling I will definitely meet the dog in my dream.

But I don't think dogs are allowed in shelters, or are they? When we are off the air I say cheerfully, "Have a great week, Chase and Mitzy!"

Chase says a cheerful goodbye back to me but Mitzy doesn't. As I start to walk off set, the new pretty yet standoffish reporter, who has only been with us a mere two weeks, decides to finally say goodbye to me. She says, "Oh, goodbye Gayle. Uh, do you mind if I give you a suggestion?"

"Why no, go ahead," I say politely, a little concerned why she would give me a suggestion about my reporting, I guess, but she begins.

"Well, your orange pant suit, uh, perhaps you don't realize that orange is not your color? It's Halloweenish looking. Orange looks better on dark-haired women like me. Isn't that the same orange pantsuit you wear on those billboards where you're holding that dog? You should wear something besides orange because of your yellowish blonde hair."

Startled, I decide to regain my composure, not walking quickly away like I want to but smiling. I say, "Thank you." I turn away. If I had eyes in the back of my head, as my late Grandmother would say, I would see maybe an astonished look on her face as my heels click walking away. I pass by Chase and realize he's heard the whole thing. He rolls his eyes, which only I can see. I smile as I continue on. Mitzy was weird and rude at the same time, but I need to try to move on because I had a psychic vibe the first moment, we met that she would not be easy to work with. It comes to me how she reminds me of Guiseppi, the rude server I met last year who ultimately changed his ways and became the star witness in the criminal case Alex and I helped solve. I wonder how he's doing?

But I must admit, in the few times I've seen Mitzy, she has been impeccably dressed and has a professional demeanor on camera. I vow not to wear my orange pantsuit again at least not to work. Maybe ever! Halloweenish is a word? Suddenly, I feel sorry for her. Alex says I feel sorry for everything, even bugs. Like how I felt sorry for Guiseppi when I met him with that sour demeanor of his. Now he is in the witness protection program because he came forward with information about the drug dealings of his former boss. His testimony saved a woman from going to jail. Go figure.

However, Alex is correct about me. I've saved many a spider, daddy long legs, cockroach, you name it. And I'm always nice to rude people and hope they someday see the light. It's easier to be kind. Anyway, was Mitzy trying to be hurtful or helpful? Hurtful probably.

Mitzy's last job let her go for reasons unknown. But she was apparently a model in Chicago and then became a reporter. I wonder why she was fired. I try not to roll over in the gossip. I have to think of the task at hand now an interview at Bay Star Shelter in an hour. Perhaps I'll really meet the dog in my dream and have a mission to follow to find another dog. Sadly, I remember Mitzy says she's allergic to dogs so Wes, my boss, asked me not to bring my little dog Magic into the studio on Sundays anymore. The Weather Dog, as everyone calls Magic now, is famous from our Sunday morning shows where she sits on a stool while I do the weather. I ask, "What do you say Magic? Will it be a great day?" Her paws go up giving me a double high five. We're on billboards around the Bay. When I meet people who recognize me, they ask about Magic. I sigh, because now, weather permitting, Wes says we can do the weather outside the studio, no stool just me and Magic in a stroller. Next week's Sunday show will be outside, weather permitting or maybe inside at Sommerset House. I'll have to ask about it today. Another Plan B moment to think about.

As I turn into my office, I can hear Mitzy call to Chase in a flirtatious way, "Bye bye, Chasey!" I think to myself, Chasey? No one here calls him that. She struts by, ignoring me. Whew, she's going to be a handful. I get my things together in my office, go into the ladies' room, and change into my jeans, red socks and sneakers and green Christmas sweatshirt. The green sweatshirt with sequined red Christmas trees is warm. I put on my red Christmas ornament earrings. I'll meet Saul, my photographer, at the shelter. I'm about to leave when my cell rings, a call coming in from a Los Angeles area code. Unknown, but I take the call anyway, just in case because my cousin and friends of mine live there.

"Hello?"

"Gayle, it's your old server, remember me? Don't say my name out loud."

"Uh hello!" Oh my gosh, I recognize his voice. It's Guiseppi! I was just thinking of him and how Mitzy reminds me of his old rude behavior. He's supposed to be in a witness protection program and not contacting anyone from his past.

I almost drop my phone. "Wow, I was just thinking of you, I thought you are, you know... away?"

"Yes, I've opted out of the program and am willing to take the risk. I'm very cautious, don't worry. I can't talk long. I'll be moving to your town before Christmas if I can but uh...."

"My town?"

"Yes, helping on that thing we did, changed everything. I'm moving there with my cousin, Gio. But I need to ask you a favor."

Without a beat I say, "Of course, what is it?" I'm flabbergasted he's going to live in Mystic Bay. Guiseppi comes right to the point. "The reason I'm calling is, well...you know you were so kind when I was a real difficult dude way back then and well, actually you changed my life forever."

"Really?"

"Yes, really, helping on that thing we did change everything." He doesn't say the criminal case.

"So, I'm wondering if you could help my younger cousin get a fresh start in town?"

"Of course, I'll help. What can I do?"

"I haven't met him in person. I just found out about him, really. Gio is my aunt Corrine's son. She gave him away at birth. He's eighteen now and he's been in foster homes all his life. Before she passed away, Aunt Corrine finally told my Aunt Talia about him. You see, our family was a broken one. My mother was not married when she passed away either. I went to live with my grandma and Aunt Talia and now miraculously, I find out I have a cousin, Giovanni. Aunt Talia told me the story and with help from the people here, I tracked him down."

"This is amazing. I'm happy for both of you."

"Thanks. We've been talking on the phone for a month and I want him to live with me, get a new start in your wonderful Mystic Bay. He's aged out of foster care and I told him about you and how angels once appeared to little kids in Mystic Bay. I want to build a new life there. You know we all need family."

"You are right about family to be sure. Is your cousin here in Mystic Bay?"

"No, today he's flying into San Francisco. He doesn't need money. I sent him enough to get here and pay for a hotel and for an apartment. I'm really lucky that I have a mentor who's helping me start a business in Mystic Bay, but that will take some time. Gio needs a job and to find an apartment. I plan to be there soon as I can so we can have Christmas together. I have a new first and last name, Gayle, and I can't wait."

"This is great." I almost say his name but don't. "Did you give Gio my number?"

"Yes, and I'll text his number to you. He'll be staying at the Airport SF Hotel. Could you meet him there? He's had two jobs in Iowa at a fast-food restaurant and a bike shop. His name is Giovanni Bartelli but they call him Gio."

I pause, thinking. "I could meet him Tuesday morning but shouldn't you be off the phone?"

"Always thinking of others, Gayle." I hear Guiseppi laugh and realize I never have heard him laugh. He sounds like my dad's old car starting. Guiseppi was the server I tipped well and responded politely to one night while I was doing detective work following a woman even though that night, he was beyond rude like Mitzy was today. Last year, way beyond my psychic expectations, Guiseppi helped seal the conviction of the drug trafficker and potential killer. I'm astounded by it all. Guiseppi wants to live in Mystic Bay? "Are you okay, really?"

"Gayle, you are the angel on earth who came my way. That's what I told Gio. I've never been so okay. I'll take my chances; we both need family and a new start in a new town. Call me Gus, I'll be calling you soon. Before I move there, I have to finish some business and buy a car. Would you be able to give Gio a call?"

"Yes, I'll call him later today. I have to go do an interview now but I wish you luck in everything." Guiseppi, now named Gus, thanks me profusely and we say goodbye.

When the phone call is over, I say out loud, "Oh no, I'm going to worry about him even more." He's supposed to be in the witness protection program. He was a twenty-something flippant waiter when I gave the disgruntled Guiseppi, a twenty-dollar tip at the bar when I was investigating a potential criminal. I had a wig on that slipped and I think he noticed, but I was as polite as a Pollyanna. Meeting him that day changed both our lives. I'm not really shocked because this kind of synchronicity of events happens to me all the time. I'll call Gio later because I have to get to at the shelter and meet a black and white dog.

Hurrying, I leave the station get into my Mustang and wish I could speed to Bay Star Shelter but instead I drive slowly. I'm pretty hyped. Guiseppi called and has a cousin Gio? Wait 'til' I tell Alex. But my mom, Marie, calls me from San Diego. "Mom, hi, I'm on my way to my interview at Bay Star Shelter. Is everything okay?"

"Yes Gayle, I had a prophetic dream something was going on with you. Is everything okay there?"

"Well, Mom, all I can tell you is my angel came to me in a dream again and this time she was holding Dukie. I'm going to meet a dog today and bring it home. The dog and I will embark on a mission to save another dog that looks like Dukie, as well as other dogs. It's really quite worrisome yet amazing."

"Yes, I guessed something big was going on. Call me later to talk about it okay? I want to hear everything about the dog. It is really happening!"

"I will, Mom." After we hang up, I think again about how the synchronicity of life truly astounds me. First, I've inherited my mother's psychic DNA, as she did before me from my grandmother, and we both have prophetic dreams. However, my dreams are angel-sent. I see my angel in my dreams. My mother's psychic tendencies accelerated as she grew older and so have mine. She, along with Alex's dad, solved the biggest missing person's case in California history. April Sorenson, a little girl went missing almost thirty years ago, and my mom worked with the San Francisco police department that included Alex's dad. It seemed like an impossibility to ever find where the little girl was. But my mom had a vision and drew a map where April might be. It dumbfounded everyone when the lost girl was found.

I find the parking garage near the shelter. Entering the shelter, I don't see a dog anywhere. Walking into the director's office, Ronna, the director of Bay Star Shelter and Tyler Parker, CEO of Sommerset House, give me the warmest of greetings. They are two unbelievably giving people. My cameraman, Saul, walks in with his equipment and I make the introductions. We begin talking about the campaign, A Christmas of Hope. I explain how Saul will take photos of us for the billboards at the end of the interview. Philanthropist, Tyler Parker, is partnering with Bay Star Shelter, to help jump-start the campaign with money needed to bring Christmas to the homeless in shelters and even more.

Last year, Alex and I went on a mission to help save Tyler's father from harm. Yes, it was my first and I thought only dream where my angel showed me a future crime I was tasked to solve. My slightly psychic vibe finally figured it all out. It was a big story in the local news. I didn't solve the case alone. With the help of Alex, the police, and some angels above, we helped save Tyler's father. But that's last year's news. Now, I have a different dream to think about. Will I meet a black and white dog today? Will the dog and I search for dogs in peril? I have to meet Gio and help him with job possibilities and a place to live. I'm anxious about it all, but have work to do.

Saul sets up his camera. We three sit in Ronna's office and a smiling older gentleman sporting an Indiana Jones hat and long white pony tail and Santa beard walks in. Introductions are made to Jerome Golightly. He looks to be around sixty, I'm guessing, "Nice to meet you, Gayle, I admire your work."

"Why thank you." Another older man with a limp comes in wearing the campaign Christmas sweatshirt. He is introduced as Vince, a man who looks weathered and melancholy.

He shakes my hand and says, "I work in the kitchen here. Hey Jerome, do you want me to feed that dog more or bring her in here? I'll take her home if you don't want her."

Jerome looks at Vince with kindness. "No, but thanks Vince, I'm going to take the dog home with me after we finish here."

"Uh, okay." Ronna then asks Vince to please get us all coffees and he leaves.

Jerome says, "Ronna, I found a dog and it was as if she was waiting for someone. No one here had seen her before."

I'm taken aback; is that the dog I'm supposed to meet? But Jerome said he's taking the dog home? Ronna starts talking. "Okay, Jerome, just be sure to take her home before lunch starts, okay?"

"Sure" he says.

Ronna turns to me, "This year at Bay Star Shelter, we are excited about your reporting Tyler Parker's generosity. Now we will have the biggest and best party ever with gifts for the kids. This Christmas is going to be exceptional thanks to Tyler Parker's involvement."

"My pleasure," Tyler smiles. As Ronna and I talk about the set up for the interview, Jerome goes out and brings more chairs in the office. I decide to say something, "Jerome, may I ask is the stray dog, black and white?"

"Why, yes she is," he says with a surprised smile.

"Ronna and Jerome, you may not know this about me, but, uh, well, my intuition told me I would take a black and white dog home from here today as odd as it sounds. Tyler knows of my abilities from last year."

Tyler Parker says, "Believe her. Remember, she's the detective who solved my father's case."

Ronna and Jerome nod their heads yes and Ronna says, "Of course, we remember it was you, please tell us what you're thinking."

I go on, "This is something I'm supposed to do. The dog will help me in the future rescue a dog and possibly others."

Jerome says, "Why how wonderful, Gayle. Would you like to see her now?"

"No, not yet, let's do the interview first." I'm discombobulated thinking about the dog but then Ken Leighton walks in the office and my heart skips a beat. Ken is a real, honest-to-goodness angel! He's a huge man of color, former coach of the San Francisco Shakers football team and owner of Heaven Can't Wait Angel

Store in Mystic Bay. He and his family live on Moon Road off Main Street, just walking distance from our house.

His caring eyes shine and he almost glows when I look at him. As we say hello, I contemplate how hard it is not to stare at him when I see him in town or like now as he shakes hands with Ronna, Tyler, and Jerome. As I introduce Saul to him, they all chat amongst themselves and I am awed by the scene I'm witnessing. An angel, living as a human, volunteers here but everyone in the room thinks he's just as human as they are? Incredible!

How do I know Ken is an angel? Well, Alex, my husband, is really half-angel. Alex hesitated to tell me as we fell in love but he finally let me know that his mother was an earth-bound angel, gone on now to heaven to be with his late father. She was sent to meet his father and live a human life with him to love and cherish him the rest of his life. He needed her. What a heavenly outcome and I wonder everyday how often it happens...angels living as humans. How many are there in the world? It's mind-blowing.

Only angels can fly so Alex, as a half-angel can't fly. His mother took him flying as a child and he explained to me the magic of flying while holding his mother's hand. Flying nights stopped, he said, when he was around five, so he always thought he dreamed that he went flying but he didn't. When Alex turned eighteen, his mom told him the truth.

Alex and I both have psychic abilities. His are inherited from his human father. His father's self-esteem was low because when he was a child people seemed to fear his ability to predict things. But when his father met his angel mother, his confidence bloomed. Not a coincidence, our parents were psychic detectives, and helped solved the April Sorenson case years ago. Sometimes I wonder why me, why us? Was the synchronicity and serendipity, written in the stars? Why are we so fortunate to know the angel secret only a few know?

Last Christmas, as midnight came, Alex and I were privileged to see the angels fly above us on the beach. Awestruck, magical, phenomenal can hardly express the amazement and the feeling. Our souls felt peace spreading over us. Wings of gossamer hues glowed in the moonlight. The angels miraculously glided above, their wings making sounds like flocks of geese in flight. As we walked home, we agreed the moment was like standing inside the pages of a fairytale.

"Gayle," Ken says. "Are you alright? We lost you there for more than a moment."

A little startled, I feel a sudden sense of peace. Sparkles of dusty light appear out of nowhere but I reply, "Yes, yes, just thinking of where to start." I ready myself explaining we will be shooting a short segment talking about the mission here at Bay Star. Plus, Saul will be taking a few photos of us for the promotions and billboard. I smooth my hair and look into the camera as Saul is ready.

"Everyone, hello, Gayle Force Knight here, reporting from San Francisco's Bay Star Shelter. I'm here with Ronna Smith, Director of the shelter, Tyler Parker, CEO of Sommerset House, and two wonderful volunteers." I introduce Jerome Golightly and former Coach Ken Leighton. We will discuss A Christmas of Hope campaign and the work that's being done to help those in need.

"First let me ask you, Ronna, what your thoughts are. This is a big Christmas project full of joy for kids and adults alike."

"Yes, it is, Gayle. I am thankful you are our spokesperson this year and so grateful to Tyler here and Sommerset House for giving us the resources to expand and help so many more in need. This Christmas program means everything. Kids will have clothes, presents and Christmas with Santa. There will be Christmas breakfast and lunch in three shifts. We can offer shelter and housing for more clients now thanks to Tyler Parker and others generosity."

"This is so great, Ronna and Tyler, wow, thank you for your enormous help. Tell us about it, please."

"Gayle, Sommerset House is all about getting people into safe environments. We are helping now with apartment housing, life skills and mental health support as well. We want to go the extra mile here for the need seems greater than ever in San Francisco. We're trying with baby steps to get people out of the streets and on a path to a fresh start. We thank all the corporations and generous donors for their support. Many people will be on the road to a changing productive life."

"It's wonderful, Tyler," I say. He explains how many small businesses, companies and individuals are signing up to help. Apartments are being readied and people are moving into reconstructed vacant buildings. "It's a steady but long process but it's necessary for change."

"This is fantastic news," I comment. We stop the first segment and Vince enters with coffees. After a few sips, we begin again. I ask Jerome, "How did you become involved with Bay Star?"

"Well, I've been volunteering here for years, mostly on weekends and holidays. I'm in charge of the Christmas celebration, decorations, and helping the children with their gifts." Jerome talks about the program on Christmas Day and the meals and Santa and gifts for all.

I turn to Ken. "This is former Coach Ken Leighton, of the San Francisco Shakers. Coach, please tell us about your history with Bay Star Shelter." Of course, Ken knows that I know he's an angel and about the other seven in town who are angels too and that I will keep the secret safe. Ken looks at me with shining brown eyes that radiate kindness.

"Gayle, it's been an honor to volunteer here. I started years ago when I was an assistant coach for the San Francisco Shakers and now we have the biggest Christmas campaign ever. I'm thrilled to do anything needed for the families. We want the kids and adults at the shelter and at other out reaches in the area to have a Merry Christmas of hope. Volunteers like me are going to work with Sommerset House and Tyler Parker to get more housing for people with all the donations of money, furniture, toys, clothing and necessities. It's a big undertaking. Gayle, most of the homeless live in dire conditions. I volunteer here with individuals and groups doing counselling to help improve self-esteem. Many ignore this population of people but I am so appreciative of Tyler's involvement and Ronna's commitment. We have a little over three weeks before Christmas Day and we can use all the help we can get."

"Ken, it really is a hope for Christmas. I will be reporting from Sommerset House every weekend until Christmas for an update. On your screen is the number to help. My station will accept donations starting today until Christmas.

I'll be reporting live here at Bay Star Shelter on Christmas Day. And Ken, you'll be here?"

"I will be here for sure."

I turn to Ronna. "Ronna, tell us your wish for your campaign."

"Gayle, I'm beyond excited for the population here because the out pouring of generosity from Tyler Parker, donors and the volunteers like Jerome and Ken."

I turn to the camera, "We need your support viewers, with anything you can give. Thank you, Ronna, Tyler, Jerome and Ken. Folks, get involved. We will be accepting donations starting today. Other sites taking items include Sommerset House, Williams Car Dealerships around the Bay Area and all public libraries in the metropolitan area. The numbers to donate are on your screen now. Let's do our part. It feels so good to give to others a hope for Christmas. It's going to be the best Christmas yet here at Bay Star Shelter."

We stop shooting and I feel good about it. Vince walks back in as we are finishing up and Saul is getting ready to take our photo. He says, "Gayle, I want to tell you my story, is that okay?"

"Of course."

"Well, I was homeless nine months back. Ronna took me in and Coach Ken here took me under his wing helping me get a fresh start. I am living in a Sommerset House apartment thanks to Tyler Parker and Jerome's help. I have a job at the shelter in the kitchen." When Vince said Ken took him under his wing, I gulped.

"Yeah, but well...there's only one other thing I want. When I saw that dog in the kitchen, I was sad because it made me think about how I want to find Buddy, my dog."

Vince looks suddenly sadder. I take in a quick breath but have to ask knowing this must be part of my mission with the dog I've yet to meet. "Vince, tell me about your dog." I already know what he will tell me. With the help of the dog in the kitchen, I am to find Vince's dog before Christmas. Will he really look like Dukie? This is surreal.

"Well, I was on the streets, like I said, months ago before I got an apartment, standing outside the grocery store. I was talking to a homeless guy I know when an old beat-up truck pulled in. A big guy got out and grabbed my Buddy, just like that. I didn't have a leash for him because Buddy had only hung around me for a few days. He just walked next to me all the time. This guy was big. He put Buddy in his truck and sped away. I tried running after the truck, but I couldn't. He took Buddy." "I'm on a project to help locate missing dogs now so let's talk in a minute after the photo shoot," I suggest.

"Okay," he says. Saul has finished setting up where we are to stand to shoot the promotion for billboards around the Bay. Jerome has come in dressed now in a Santa suit. His hair is down to his shoulders and his beard is quite stunningly white, really Santa-looking. We position ourselves to take the photo with Santa in the middle, Ronna and Tyler on either side of him and Ken and me at each end. I smile but feel nervous. I'm about to meet the black and white dog from my dream.

After we finish the shoot, I am hugged by Tyler and Ronna. I thank Saul and he and I decide we will edit later on our computers. Ken and Jerome and I walk into the kitchen area. I know undoubtedly, the dog will help me search for Vince's missing dog, Buddy.

Jerome says to me, "I know you'll love this sweet girl, she really needs a home, Gayle."

"Jerome, would it be alright if I take the dog home?"

"Sight unseen?"

"Yes, I'm meant to take her."

"Yes of course," Jerome replies. "You are a special lady, an advocate for others and of course, an advocate for our blessed animals."

"She surely is," says Ken.

The smell of spaghetti wafts in the air. The chef, Vince and staff are preparing the lunch meal. We say hello to all. But my eyes go to the corner. Sitting on a small rug is the furry, precious black and white dog exactly as I saw in my dream. She seems a few years old and covered with black fur with patches of white. Her eyes catch mine and they seem sad, yet sparkle like the sun is shining on her. Her dirty fur reminds me of the dark mountains of Big Bear where we skied last weekend. Looking out the window at the moonlit scene, the patches of snow glowed with sparkles like tiny stars on the cold winter mountains. It's then her name comes to me. Moonlight on powdery white snow in winter. Winter. It's a beautiful name for a special dog with love in her eyes. All dogs radiate love and my heart melts.

Winter stands and walks over to me just as in my dream I lean down and pet her. I carefully pick her up feeling she's too light and should weigh more. Cuddling her feels like I've had her always in my arms. "I'll name her Winter. Her fur looks like snow on Big Bear at night." "I love her name," says Ken. "What a heavenly image and what a heaven-sent dog!"

I smile knowing he's an angel. Does he know of my dream, I wonder. Oh, if the others only knew.

Jerome adds, "It is a sweet name for such a sweet lady." Winter wags her tail. They all come to pet her. I say, "She's underweight, Ken."

He replies, "We have to get her to the vet hospital today before you take her home. I'll call Jordana.

"Yes, thank you. I have a blanket in my car. Will you walk me to my car?"

"Of course,"

Ken's wife is an angel too and part of our two-angel vet team at Beach Tails Animal Hospital in Mystic Bay. The other angel vet is Josh. Yes, that in itself sounds like fantasy or a miracle dream, yet it's true. Their healing hands are known throughout the town but townsfolk think they are only amazing animal healers, not angels. If they only knew...

"Thanks again, Gayle, for taking Winter home," Jerome says with such joy on his face. Vince comes over to pet Winter and says, "It's nice you're taking her home. I wish you could find Buddy." He hands me a piece of paper. "Here's my cell number just in case."

Jerome looks at Vince and says in a kind way, "Vince, maybe we can all look for him but remember you just had Buddy for a little while like you did all the others." Others? I wonder what that means and how I will find the dog but it's something I'm meant to do.

"What does Buddy look like? Do you have a photo of him?"

"No photo though he's sort of tan medium like a German Shepherd." Amazing, I think Dukie was a shepherd mix.

"I'll look out for him, Vince, and let you know."

"Thanks. Will you call the police because they wouldn't help me."

"No, I'll use my intuition and look on the internet at shelters." Vince says okay and goes back to his work.

Jerome bends down and kisses Winter on her head. "Have joy, my Winter. I hope to see you again."

We say our final goodbyes and Ken walks me to my car. I'm still holding Winter so I settle her in the front seat and get in the driver side. Ken says, "Go right to Beach Tails Animal Hospital. I'll meet you there."

"Thank you, Ken. I do have something else to ask you."

"Of course," Ken says. His eyes glow like star shine.

"I know two cousins who are coming to town to live. If you still have the apartment available above your store, I would love for them to see it."

Ken says, "Sure, tomorrow, I'm in the store. Please bring them by if you can."

"Terrific, I hope to bring Gio, one of the cousins, over to meet you. I'm meeting him for the first time in the morning, hopefully. "

We say we will see each other in a little while and I drive away with a wave, realizing I just had the longest conversation ever with Ken. Since Alex and I saw Ken and the other angels fly down the beach last Christmas night, I've been avoiding them all in town, really because I'm in such awe. It's still unbelievable. I've seen their luminous wings, and their glow each time we meet now. I know their presence has changed my whole life. I knew there were angels; after all, I see one in my dreams. Alex is half-angel, and that's why I am privy to the knowledge they live among us.

Alex's angel mother told him the secret years ago. but we didn't know they were in our town until the flight of angels last year.

She told Alex that angels who live as humans grow old just as we do. Then, when it's time, they go back to their heavenly realm to be with those who have passed on. Thinking about this brings me comfort. Alex told me the angels manifest as humans sometimes to guide and help people understand gratitude for the sweetness of life but also to learn to cope with the hard times. I know, I'm just an ordinary woman with a slightly psychic vibe, but I get to be part of this miraculous knowledge!

Changing my thoughts to Gus and Gio, I hope they'll be able rent the apartment above Ken's angel store. The guys unknowingly will meet an angel. Who would have guessed that in the town I always wanted to move back to, I'd marry a half-angel and get to know real angels living human lives!

The car is nice and warm for Winter as I call my husband. She has settled down on the blanket and looks at me with sleepy eyes. I know she must so tired. "You won't believe this Alex!" I tell him the whole angel and Dukie dream I had last night and all that's happened, including Winter, Vince's lost dog, Buddy, and how I hope somehow Winter will help me find Buddy. "I'm bringing Winter to the animal hospital now. Ken is meeting me. Can you meet me there?" Alex is utterly bowled over.

"Yes, this is beyond surreal. There's always room for one more dog at our house. Can't wait to meet her."

After we say goodbye and as I drive the rest of the half hour home, I reflect on my dream. I dreamed of Winter exactly as she looks, and Dukie communicated that she would help me find a dog that looked like him. Maybe even other dogs. Alex is right. It is beyond surreal. But Dukie, my dog in heaven's realm, wants me to bring Winter home and find Buddy.

Driving along, the bright sun is shining noon-time high on the chilly way to Mystic Bay. I have to keep my eyes on the road but glance at Winter again. Her eyes meet mine. She has a look of gratefulness yet sadness. Where did she come from? What's her story? So many sad stories for the homeless families and animals on the streets, all in need. The dogs and cats wandering everywhere all just want a place to call home but they can't ask for help. They can only once in a great while stand at a door hoping someone may let them in.

The realization that Winter was sent to me by an angel and my late Dukie, fills my heart. Our dog, Magic, came to my door one night last year, sent by Alex's angel mother, we know now. We're sure his mother wanted us to meet in the kismet of our lives, woven together like my grandmother's crocheted blankets. Little did I know then that I would meet Alex solving a case, a crime that fortunately never happened. The tapestry of love weaves along in my life. Will Alex and I embark on a new adventure with Winter to find the German Shepherd-type dog Vince named Buddy? Ken said he will help in any way he can. But how can I ask a real angel to help us? I don't know that I can.

When I lie in bed at night in need of a heavenly answer, so many times an answer comes to me. But this is different. Ken helping us is unreal but such a magnificent thought. Then another thought floats in as clear as today's robin's-egg-blue sky. Will I dream where Buddy is? Of course, and Ken will fly to help if I need him. Oh, how magical it will be, a Christmas mission! Almost as if Winter understands my thoughts, she looks up at me and I look into her brown shining eyes. In my mind, I see us surrounded by dogs. More dogs to rescue? The image leaves as I turn down Main Street and on to the animal hospital.

Chapter 3
The Extraordinary

When Winter and I meet Alex at Beach Tails, they immediately bond. "Can't wait to take you home, Winter." I can tell Alex's whisper calms her. Ken's wife, Doc Jordana, is a beautiful raven-haired angel, it's true. But her beauty is in her angel soul and her healing touch. She and Ken helped a group of volunteers, rescue dozens of horses that now reside in a ranch on the edge of town. They are happy and live in a peaceful setting for the rest of their lives. Just as all living creatures should be.

Winter's eyes look at Jordana with gratitude. Like many rescued animals, it's as if they understand they are safe now. Doc Jordana examines Winter. "She is about two years old but needs to put on at least ten pounds of weight."

Alex and I watch in awe as Jordana uses her healing touch to make the sore on Winter's back leg start to heal. She gives her some immunizations and Winter licks Jordana's hands. She carefully washes Winter with warm wet towels and Winter's eyes close, loving the warmth and the fluffy dry towel. Jordana says, "Ken told me about your dream, Gayle, and how you came to find this wonder of a dog. She'll need to be spayed after Christmas, but we'll wait until then since she needs to gain weight and you and Winter have a mission. She is indeed fortunate that Jerome found her. It clearly was a heaven-sent meant-to-be."

"Thank you, Jordana. We are so happy to take her into our furry family."

Ken comes into the office as we are leaving. A smile on his angelic face gives me peace. He says, "Winter is in good hands. Please know Jordana and I will help you if you need anything." Jordana's smile is warm and she reminds us there is no charge for first exams and shots for all rescue dogs at the Beach Tails Animal Hospital. We take Winter home with thankful words to both.

When we get home, Alex takes Winter through the gate to the back yard. I walk in the front door to over-the-top-kisses and hugs. Welcoming me with his usual response, Maurice jumps on me when I bend down to pet Ralph and Magic. Is it jealousy or playfulness? I think a little of both. I let the animals out to the backyard to meet their new pal.

With wonder, I witness what my angel must have known. Winter is a magnet to animals. They walk up slowly sniffing her and then Ralph and Magic roll on their backs for Winter to know they instantly love her. Even Maurice goes nose-to-nose with Winter for a moment. Winter gives him a little lick. "This is quite amazing," Alex says, putting his arm around me. Magic gets up from the ground and stands like a circus dog on her hind legs prancing toward Winter. This is what she does for our mail carrier, Bill, when she hears his truck come down the street in the morning. She whines and we instantly go outside the front door with her. She hops on two legs to Bill's truck and he gives her a dog treat. He gives all the dogs on his route treats. Our friend Jamie Bond says that when Bill comes to his store, his dog, Bondo, goes nuts running in circles. He runs up to Bill like he hasn't seen him in months, and spins.

Alex says sighing, "They all instantly love her." Magic drops down and nuzzles Winter while Ralph and Maurice lay down next to her.

I say, "Look at her soft presence, her calmness, her ease with them. Will she be like this as we search for Buddy?"

"Absolutely. Look at her. It's her calling. Winter come to me," says Alex. As she walks to him her head is low. Is it from her past on the streets? "Alex, she must know her name, already. That's extraordinary." Alex picks her up and she licks his face. "My pretty Winter," he whispers.

We go inside and stay awhile in our living room, with the new addition to the pack fitting in nicely. I call Aunt Nancy and Uncle Dick, who live next door to us, telling them about Winter. They are intrigued and will come over tomorrow to stay with her when I leave for work for a few hours and then meet Gio. I call my dearest friend, Maggie, to tell her about Winter. She is the town's most blessed clairvoyant and senses angels near many times. Maggie was with the anonymous child with special needs who saw an angel a few years ago. The child said her first word that day. The word was "angel."

Maggie's abilities have grown and she is seeing angels now, glimpsing their presence as her great grandmother did before her. The late great Madam Norma saw angels near but didn't speak of it while alive. Her spirit came to Ken and asked him to write a book about her life called *The Woman Who Saw Angels*. Ken's book is in the Angel Museum in Riverton. No one ever guesses he's an angel himself. Along with Ken's book are the accounts in a documentary about the angels appearing to the three children. It was filmed by Noah, Maggie's' writer husband.

Maggie tells me how truly extraordinary the angel dream was. "You will find Buddy; I know you will. I can't wait to meet Winter."

I tell her I'll call her tomorrow and we say goodnight. Everyone needs a friend like Maggie.

I call my mom and we chat more about Winter and finding Buddy. "My heart tells me you will find Buddy, Gayle. You will find him before we arrive on the twenty-third. We've decided to stay with Nancy and Dick as you and Alex have your hands full."

"Okay Mom. Yes, we have more animals here than most!" We laugh and hang up and I remark to myself how blessed I am to have my family. As the sunsets with its orange and pink glow on Mystic Bay's heart-shaped harbor, and the dogs and cat are fed, Alex's says, "Since I took off my boot, I'll make us my famous grilled cheese and tomato sandwiches."

"Great idea, I'm glad you're better!" While he cooks, we talk of the day. We are famished after the emotional day. When finished eating we retire to sit in the living room, and Ralph plunks down in his dog bed while Magic and Maurice curl up on the couch with me. Sitting in his big red chair, Alex picks up Winter and brings her to his lap. She lays her head on his arm.

It's then I go into detail of the weird and pretty rude exchange with Mitzy Blane, Vince at the shelter and the call from Guiseppi who is now calling himself Gus.

"Well, this is something. Guiseppi out of the Witness Protection Program? That's a scary thought for him and he wants to move here? Are you going to call his cousin?"

"Right now." I pick up my phone. "I'm going to ask him to meet me for breakfast tomorrow after I go to the station."

Gio answers.

"Hello, Gio? This is Gayle Knight. Guiseppi, I mean Gus, your cousin, asked me to call you."

"Hi," he says in almost a whisper.

"Welcome to the Bay Area. Gus tells me you will be moving here to Mystic Bay with him and I'd like to take you to breakfast tomorrow, if I may. I have some ideas on a place for you two to live as well as how to help you find jobs."

I hear him say, in an almost inaudible voice, "Yes, Gayle, my"... and then I can't understand what he's saying. "Excuse me, we must have a bad connection so could you say that again?"

In a louder voice he says, "Where shall I meet you?"

"The restaurant at your hotel is really good. Let's meet there at nine and then I'll take you to Mystic Bay to see an apartment and go into some businesses that need help. I have some ideas."

Gio is very polite and thanks me. I say goodbye thinking I should have told him what I look like and ask him what he looks like. But I'll find him, I'm sure.

Feeling a sense of sorrow in Gio as I did Guiseppi, I think about his childhood mirroring Giuseppe's. No parents to turn to and in Gio's case, only foster homes. I explain to Alex, "I'm meeting Gio tomorrow. He talks so low I could hardly understand him."

"I'm sure you will help him. Look how things change in one day. This has been one amazing Sunday."

"So, it has." As the evening goes on, we talk more about how Winter will be by my side as I look for Buddy. "Gayle, it's coming to me just as it did to your mom and Maggie, that you will discover the exact location to find Buddy in your dreams."

"I hope so. He's not far, I feel that too. I'll check all the rescue organizations. I'll call Andy Walin now to see if he has room at his rescue."

"That would be wonderful."

Calling Andy sets the whole operation in motion. I'm hoping to get some clues. I tell Alex, "If necessary, I will drive around one day on my own, hoping to sense anything. I'll look in all the rescue data bases and alert them about Buddy to call either you or me."

"You and Winter must be exhausted and I have an early meeting tomorrow so, let's take our critters to bed and dream of angels, shall we?"

While dusk turns to night, we go out to the patio. From the side yard we can feel the chilly wind pick up and watch the lights of the boats in the harbor gently moving. The air smells sweet and salty at the same time. The clouds are still visible.

In our garden the flowers and birds are sleeping. We marvel at the way Winter resembles the Pied Piper as the dogs and cat follow her around the yard. We sit for a while and admire the night stars appearing, seemingly popping out one by one. When sleep calls, we go in settling down in our bedroom. I feel happy putting a new dog bed down for Winter by the other dog beds, near our own. From the bedroom doorway, she looks at me with those sweet eyes but turns and walks back to the living room. I follow. The other dogs and cat are already snug in our room, but I'm tuning in to the spirit of this dog as she lays once again in the bed by the fireplace. I go over to her and pet her fluffy fur. "You want to stay here tonight? You must like this bed and Christmas blanket. Maybe it reminds you of a home you once loved. It's okay." Somehow, I feel she understands my words, at least the cadence. "Goodnight sweet Winter." I pet her once more and go into our bedroom. Already asleep, Alex and the animals breathing should lull me to sleep but I find myself thinking of the day.

Winter wants to stay in the living room. Is she waiting for someone? My intuition doesn't say no, so I ask the angels but I hear only a thought in my mind: "*Just love her.*" The angel's whisper has calmed me. I think of the extraordinary day. At work, I was not anticipating rudeness from Mitzy. I immediately have a vision of her face with a stern expression, then as quickly as it appeared, I feel sadness in her soul. Then Gus comes to mind. It's incredibly ironic that he called me and wants to move here with his long-lost cousin. Then another irony or a meant-to-be happenstance at Bay Star Shelter; the dog Winter came home with me, the dog in my angel dream with Dukie. I know he's helping me from heaven's realm.

My eyes become heavy. Silently, I ask the angels to please help me find Buddy. I see a misty vision of him in my mind. Is he scared? I know A Christmas of Hope will help so many and perhaps I can help this dog I'm destined to find. I drift off, thankful for my abilities so similar to my mother's. But as I drift, I wonder how Winter will help me.

Chapter 4
Gio Comes To Town

Gio's the spitting image of a younger Gus, I note, as he walks in the restaurant. However, he lacks the arrogance I saw in his cousin's face the first time I met Guiseppi at a bar. Yet Gio's eyes are the same deep brown and his wavy black hair is slicked back in Guiseppi fashion. His demeanor seems shy and nervous, but I get nervous myself meeting strangers the first time. He wears a black sweatshirt, jeans, and tennis shoes. He half-smiles at me as if he knows who I am, and I stand and wave from the booth. I have my hair down but under a ball cap and no TV make-up. I have to keep a low profile, as some people recognize me when I'm out with my standard TV look, a blond ponytail. Today, I don't want to be recognized.

Gio walks up to me with a slight smile and says so softly, "Hello." We shake hands.

"I'm Gayle. Please sit down. It's nice to meet you."

Gio responds, "Me too." I can tell his nervousness is leaving some as he sits down. I sure hope I can help him.

There's a coffee thermos on the table so I pour myself a second cup, since I arrived early. "Would you like coffee?" He nods. As I pour, I say smiling, "Let's order breakfast. I'm starving, are you?"

"Yes," he says quietly. I almost have to read his lips. Gio is a super-soft-talking young man. We sip our coffee in silence and I raise my hand when I see the female server look at us, hopefully suggesting to her that we need to order. But I don't think she liked that I was in the booth for fifteen minutes before ordering. The place is crowded. She comes over and man, does she have a frown like an upside-down smile. Her name tag says Sydney, and as she looks at Gio, I see an interest in her eyes. Then she looks at me. "What will you have?" I note her name on her badge.

I say, looking at the menu, "Let's see Sydney, I'll have the pancake special and could we have another thermos of your great coffee, please?"

Sydney gives me a dirty look. "You drank that fast."

"It's great coffee," I smile.

Maybe she thinks I'm rude. You know, I seem to attract grumpy servers, like Gus was when I first met him. Sydney curtly says to me, "I'll bring you another thermos of coffee. It takes four minutes, Mrs., and I'm busy." Without a chance for me to respond, she immediately turns to Gio, changing her tone to a gentle one. "Uh, your order sir?"

Gio doesn't look at her but at the menu. It sounds funny when he says, "Um jeez and him." He spoke in almost a whisper.

"What?" says the server.

In a louder voice Gio says, "Omelet, cheese and ham."

But rude Sydney doesn't seem to mind his soft voice. She smiles and the biggest frown turns into almost a pretty smile.

She looks back at me with a frown again and off she goes.

"Your voice is so soft. I could hardly hear you."

"I know," he says in a louder voice. "I know and I am trying to work on it."

He's looking out the window at the parking lot. I sense sadness.

He turns to look at me and still with a soft voice he says, "You look like the billboard right outside here next to the highway. You're with a cute dog. Is it your dog?"

Yes, that's my dog, Magic."

"I love dogs and Gus says we'll get one as soon as we can."

"Right now, I'm looking for a lost dog for a friend and I may need some help. Do you think you might be interested in helping me?"

"Yes," he says softly, "I would. Maybe I'll even find a dog for us."

"I'll help you guys for sure."

He whispers, "Gus said we would love living in your town and you wouldn't mind helping me because you are the nicest person he ever met."

"That's kind of him to say. I saw a good person in him and I see that same goodness in you too. I'd like to help you in any way I can, so I made some calls this morning and I actually have possible jobs for you to interview for and an apartment for you and Gus to see. I'd like to take you to Mystic Bay today to see the town and meet the shopkeepers and tour the apartment. It's right on Main Street above a store. Is that okay?"

In a louder voice, "Really? That would be great."

"Today I called my friend, Jamie Bond, who owns Bondo Bikes and he says he needs part-time help for sure through Christmas. He has a small room and bath in the back of his shop and if he hires you, you could stay there for free until we can find an apartment for you."

His eyes light up and he says softly. "This is amazing. Gus said you are an angel. I need jobs until we get the business going."

"That's sweet of him. But that's not all, another job has opened up. Laurjean and her husband Donnie own The Next Door Café. They need part-time help too. What do you say?"

"I can't thank you enough." Gio is smiling and his voice is much louder.

"Great. After breakfast, check out from the hotel and we'll drive to Mystic Bay. We'll stop in at both Bondo's Bikes and The Next Door Café and right across the street from the bike shop is the apartment I want you to see. It's above my friend Ken's store, Heaven Can't Wait. If for some reason you don't get the job at Bondo's Bikes, you can stay with us."

"Thank you so much!"

Of course, I can't tell Gio that Ken is truly an angel. I do explain Ken's store sells everything angel plus Ken's the former coach of The San Francisco Shakers football team.

"Really? He's the coach that helped the team with sportsmanship. Before he came, they were a messed-up team my foster dad said. He thinks Coach Ken changed the NFL. Wait until I tell him."

"That's great. You'll like all the people you meet today and now we have a plan and you have a place to stay until an apartment is available."

"Gus sent me money for a down payment and I have some of my own money too. I really appreciate this."

"I'm happy to help. You'll love Mystic Bay. The people are friendly and welcoming." I glance out of the window, thinking of Winter and how I have a big feeling we'll be on a mission soon. Is it only a dream away?

His voice becomes softer again, "Gus said you are a very psychic and spiritual. He told me I need to tell you my angel story."

"Intrigued I say, "Please do." I put my coffee cup down to listen. Sydney, the grumpy server, brings the refilled coffee thermos and plunks it down without a word. Gio waits until she is out of earshot. He looks down as I fill his cup then mine. "I was adopted as a baby but the couple had problems and divorced. I was given back to the state and put in the foster care system when I was four. I don't remember my adopted parents but I have their last name. They gave me up just like that. When I was young, in two different homes, I always thought someday my real biological mom would come find me because she missed me. But she never did."

"I'm sorry." My heart aches for him. "That must have been so hard."

"Well, what happened was, when I was about seven, I thought I was dreaming but I wasn't. I saw an older lady stand at the end of my bed. She had an accent and she told me she loved me and everything would be okay. I wasn't scared, just not sure of my eyes. Was the woman really real? She was gone like that." He snaps his fingers. "The next day, I was sent to live in a much better foster home.

"The people, the Banners, were very nice to me. I stayed there eleven years. When I turned eighteen a few months ago, I knew I would be out of the system. They had to let another foster child come live with them and share the bedroom with the foster boy I roomed with. But the Banners wanted me to stay and sleep on the couch. They said I was part of the family. They suggested I keep working at my job at the bike store to help with the expenses like food as long as I needed to but to save for my schooling or an apartment. I was looking at getting a scholarship somewhere but I really didn't like school. They loved my cooking. I cooked a lot of the meals on a budget."

"How nice. They must be kind people and you must be a great cook." My heart is breaking for this sweet guy who is opening up to me.

"Three weeks ago, I knew I was going to leave, but I didn't know where. The Banners had given me some money as a birthday present. They said they really wanted me to stay for a while but I knew it was hard on them with an extra person now in the small house. I was unable to sleep, and a miracle happened. That night, as I lay on the couch, I felt someone kiss my forehead. I woke up and saw that older lady again by the couch I was sleeping on. I rubbed my eyes, making sure it was real. She called me by name. She said, "Giovanni, your life will be good. I love you." She smiled and then in an instant she was gone again.

"Amazingly, the next day my cousin, Gus, called the Banners. He and my Aunt Talia were searching for me and he found out where I was with help from people he knows. He was looking up birth records in Chicago. The name Giovanni Bellini caught his eye and it showed the same year I was born. Giovanni, he told me, was my great grandfather's name. They were so happy to find me.

Gus lived with our grandma 'til she died when he was ten and with Aunt Talia all his childhood. Gus's other aunt, Corrine, was my mother. She had recently passed away. Our Aunt Talia told him that eighteen years ago, when I was born, my mother had gone away for a while. She didn't tell Aunt Talia about me until years later when she became ill. When she died, my aunt told Gus. It was a secret my mother kept for all those years. My grandmother wasn't alive when I was born.

"Gus promised he would find me and Aunt Talia is so happy now. Gus and I are going to Illinois to see her after we get our business off the ground."

"This is wonderful, Gio. You have a family. Who do you think the lady was that visited you?"

My intuition knows what he's about to say.

"When I told Gus about the lady who came two times, years apart, and what she said and how she kissed me when I was sleeping, he texted me a photo. The old lady I described was our Grandma Maria. Grandma was from Italy and a wonderful cook. Her father was named Giovanni. Gus said she came to see me to let me know her love was all around me. Gus loved her. He found out that my mother left me at a fire station with my name, pinned on a blanket. The adopted family kept Giovanni as my name, and I'm so grateful. Gus said he thinks an angel sent Grandma to me."

"A miracle of love it is. Your Grandma Maria's loving spirit came to you twice."

"Yes, I feel her love, I really do all the time. Gus told me he never had siblings and didn't know many of his family. He said he helped with a big case here and had to go away for a while."

Gio is looking at his coffee cup, then he looks up at me intently.

"You have a sad story but such a happy ending too." He nods and I see tears form in his eyes.

"Gus said you helped him become a better man."

"I don't know about that, but I do know Gus always has been a good person and ultimately was instrumental sending a criminal to jail and solving the case we were on."

"Is he in trouble? He said he had to change his name. He has a new social security card and everything."

"He's safe, he told me, and he's excited to move to Mystic Bay and start a new life with you."

Gio says, "I can't wait to meet him." I'm about to respond but our unpleasant server, Sydney arrives with our food. She plunks it down on my side but gently puts Gio's plate down. I intuitively realize she thinks I'm an older married woman with a younger guy and it's making her annoyed. I smile at her and her look reminds me of Gus' when I first smiled at him. The hostility was palpable.

"Thank you, Sydney." She walks away quickly.

As we eat, I tell Gio about the town, the people, the beach and most important-ly that children with special needs saw angels there. Three children, each with a disability, had angels come to them. One little girl said "angel," her first word. The second a little boy drew pictures of angels that looked as if a French impressionist had done the drawings. The third was a boy with a visual disability. But he was an exceptional pianist at his young age and one night, the angels came and whispered a song to him. The boy memorized it and played. It's a very famous song now. All these incidents are chronicled in The Angel Museum in Riverton."

Gio's awed by it all. "It's wonderful. Angels must have sent my Grandma Maria to me."

"Indeed, she was heaven-sent. I'll take you to the Angel Museum in Riverton, the town next to ours, where the exhibit is. They show a documentary made by a friend of ours, of the miraculous story."

"This town is special."

"It truly is."

As we finish eating and end our breakfast, I ask him when he'll be talking to Gus next but he's not sure.

The server plops the bill down in front of me and I take it. Speaking in a louder voice, Gio amazes me when he says, "Miss, this lady is changing my life, helping me get a job and a new start. You should've been nicer to her."

This was unexpected and I'm shocked but so is Sydney. She doesn't say anything, just takes my credit card and turns away, walking briskly, perhaps embarrassed.

"Gio. Thank you." He smiles a big smile and says, "You're welcome."

Of course, when she brings the card and check back, she carefully puts it on the table without a word. I say, "Thank you." When she is gone, I give moody Sydney a nice tip. Maybe she's got some sadness in her life that makes her irritable. A big tip is what angels in town would do. Wouldn't they?

Chapter 5
A Winter's Tale

It's been a long day. Gio took both jobs at Bondo Bikes and The Next Door Café. Jamie was delighted meeting him and Bondo Bikes is a good part-time fit for him. "Hey, I love your dog," says Gio.

""Yes," said Jamie. "Bondo changed my life, as did a lot of people here in town. I used to be so afraid of dogs and didn't believe in angels. I'll tell you the story tonight. I'll take you out for pizza. You can put your things in the back room and stay as long as you need to."

I felt so glad, and as if Gio has been given more than he ever hoped for. Laurjean and Donnie owners of the café, were impressed with him as well. Donnie is another one of Mystic Bay's angels, I might add. Alex and I saw him fly with the others last Christmas. I'm always in awe when I see them all in town. "You're hired," said spunky Laurjean. "Seven to two are your hours and you can work at Bondo Bikes in the afternoons. Sound good?"

"Yes ma'am. Thank you," said Gio, with new confidence.

Next, I took him over to see Ken and the apartment. Gio didn't see the glow around Ken but I did. Gio was enthusiastic about the apartment and Ken made him feel at ease of course as he showed him around. The two-bedroom place is perfect for the cousins.

Looking out the big window at the view, Gio exclaimed, "This view looks like it should be on a postcard!"

Ken said laughing, "People say that about this whole place. Gio, this town is on postcards all around town." So, Ken and Gio agreed as soon as Gus arrives, they'll sign the papers and move in. Ken said he had an extra couch in his storage unit and a table with four chairs they could have. Gio thanked Ken and told him how his foster dad loves the San Francisco Shakers football team and how Mr. Banner especially admires Ken's coaching abilities. Ken, as he does always, was appreciative and humble.

When I arrived home, all the animals except Winter ran up to me. Winter was lying by the fire and looked at me with soulful eyes. Her tail wagged but she didn't move.

"She's exhausted," My Aunt Nancy tells me. "Why she slept all day until you just came home."

I bend down to pet her. "Rest, sweet Winter. Thank you. I appreciate you dog sitting today."

"Why, sure," Aunt Nancy says. It's her favorite response. She leaves and I get supper ready for the dogs. When Alex arrives home, Winter finally gets up. She stretches. "According to Aunt Nancy, she's had a long winter's nap. No pun intended."

I share all the goings-on of a wonderful day with Gio and the things coming together for the nice deserving guy. I tell him how friendly everyone was to him and also how amazed Gio was by Jamie, Laurjean and Donnie's hiring him on the spot. "The apartment is perfect for the two cousins. He told me he felt so lucky for everything including Ken's kindness too. He's going to stay in the room at Bondo's Bike's for free until Gus arrives. He'd never seen the ocean before and could hardly look away."

"Looking at the ocean is like glimpsing heaven," Alex remarks.

"Oh, and at The Next Door Café, we had soup for lunch and the cute new server, Hope, caught his eye. I could tell. She reminded me of a younger version of Laurjean."

"This is so great, Gayle!"

"Laurjean had a large streak of green in her new short new bob. Following her lead, Hope had a green streak in her long ponytail.

"Also, Gio showed Jamie how fast he could change a bike tire. By the way, he's offered to help me find Vince's dog. Gio thanked me and Jamie's taking him out for pizza tonight. It's working out perfectly."

As the evening goes on, Winter looks at me with love in those brown eyes of hers. Yet sadness is there. "I missed you," I tell her. "I miss all my dogs and cat." I sit on the couch and Winter looks at me from her bed by the fire, but Ralph, Magic, and Maurice have to share as much of my arms and lap as possible. I ask Winter to come and jump on the couch too, but she stays put. I wonder to myself when Winter might want to come to me here on the couch. *"It's only been a moment she's been here,"* an angel whispers in my mind. Kind Aunt Nancy left a macaroni casserole for us. We eat and then sit by the fire, gazing at the four animals. Ralph curls up in his bed, and Magic and Maurice jump on my lap. Alex picks Winter up and puts her on his lap. He and I talk again about Gio and Gus. "It's beyond belief. I pray Gus will be okay. Someone is helping him start a business here. I didn't ask who it is."

Alex says, "I'm glad he's changed his identity. He'll have to stay under the radar for sure. But Mystic Bay is a good place for another secret to be kept. No one but a very few of us know angels live as humans here. It's the biggest secret in the world."

My eyes close as I listen because I'm exhausted from the last two days. I hear Alex say, "I wonder what business he's opening and where. There are a few vacant stores."

"We'll wait 'til he tells us. Who would have thought he'd choose our town, just because one night, I gave a disgruntled Guiseppi a smile and a big tip."

"It's because you are my angel." I open my eyes to see my husband. "No, you're really the angel!"

Alex says, "Look at the miracle of it all. Gus is opening a business. The former rude server not only becomes a compelling witness who put a criminal away in jail, but has the courageous gumption to start a new life here after finding his cousin. It's angel's work, Gayle, and you inspired Gus."

I laugh remembering the moment. Gus, aka Guiseppi, had such an annoyed look on his face when he was my server at the bar and restaurant a criminal owned. But I tipped him well, just like I over-tipped the disgruntled server, Sydney. A smile and some kindness changed everything.

We've always surmised Gus overheard talk about me after I left the bar. Those criminals decided I was an amateur investigator. Gus must have become worried about my involvement and came forward to the police with evidence that changed the case. Tyler's father wasn't harmed in the end.

"The outcome could have ended so differently," Alex says, "Gus is indeed brave!"

"Well Alex, maybe the butterfly effect does exist. One choice can make all the difference. But I think it wasn't my kindness to Gus that changed him. I think he must have had an epiphany, a divine intervention."

"I agree."

I'm falling asleep, so Alex suggests we get ready for bed, first taking the animals outside. The stars are shining but it's cold and silent except for the sound of the waves in the harbor. We see Aunt Nancy and Uncle Dick's bedroom light shut off. We see the moon float behind the clouds. As we walk back in the house, sweet Winter, goes to her bed by the fireplace again. Alex has coaxed her to come into our room but she has ignored him. She doesn't want to sleep in our room in the cozy bed we put out for her. We always sleep with our companion animals in our room. Suddenly, another feeling of sadness comes to me. Winter is waiting for someone to come for her. I drift off, wondering if she is waiting to help us find Buddy so her mission will be accomplished. Then she'll go back to her home, wherever that is, or perhaps someone will come find her. A tear falls on my pillow. Alex has fallen asleep and I get up once more to check on her. The animals are cozy with eyes closed as I tiptoe into the living room. By the light in the kitchen, I see Winter peacefully sleeping. The gas fireplace is on low and in the embers glow, I wonder, somehow, if Winter has wings tucked under her silky soft fur.

Chapter 6

In The Nick Of Time

Yesterday was a good day. Winter rested all day. I took Magic and Ralph to dog beach after Magic hopped on back legs for Bill the mail carrier. It's always a hoot as he laughs and gives Ralph and Magic a treat. But today, I'm awake early. It's before five am and I remember my dream. Winter, Alex and I were helping a dog come out of a big drainage pipe. I get up and go into the living room. Winter is standing by the front door and looks at me as if she knows what I know. There is a mission for us today. She wags her tail. She doesn't follow me to the bedroom to dress. I know, intuitively, we have to drive towards an area beyond Riverton, and soon. I didn't see people in the dream just a dog in a drainage pipe. How will I find it and how will Winter help? Is Winter really a Pied Piper angel dog? I think this must be the case. As I dress in jeans, t-shirt and heavy sweatshirt, I know it's cold outside so I grab more blankets for the car. Should I wake Alex? I sit, putting my socks and tennis shoes on. But Alex comes into the bathroom and I share the dream with him and how Winter and I must go. He asks, "How do you know she knows where to go and what you are doing?"

"I just do."

"I'm going with you."

"But you need to get to work for a meeting at seven."

Alex insists he will follow in his car. As he gets dressed, I let all the dogs and Maurice out, then feed them. I put food in a bag, a bowl, and bottled water in the car. Winter jumps in the passenger side just like she knows what we are doing, trying to find a dog in a drain. Alex assures the other animals we'll be back and we set off in our cars. I lead us out the driveway turning down sleepy Main Street to where I wonder. No one is about except Laurjean unlocking the front door of

The Next Door Café. She waves seeing our two cars drive by. I wave but have to concentrate. Where am I going? Please lead me, dear angels. I drive down Main Street toward the edge of town. The misty air will break soon. Driving past Andy's Rescue, I know I will need Andy's assistance today. Andy's Rescue has helped many rescued animals find homes. I've known him since a childhood camp I went to when I stayed with Aunt Nancy and Uncle Dick each summer. I will need to text Jordana if we indeed find a dog. But will it be Buddy? I couldn't see the dog in the pipe clearly.

I drive down Rt. 44 and turn left on Lonely Ridge Road as it heads east. With its many curves, it becomes a bit more dangerous to drive. In my rear view mirror, I see my loyal husband behind me and I so appreciate his steadfast love and support. Of course, he has his own gift of intuition, and if he thought we would encounter an unsafe situation, he would have told me. My intuition about the location keeps me driving for a few more miles. One abandoned farm on the left with no lights on makes me feel a sudden sadness. The orange ball of the sun's ray's inches up in the east, and I marvel at the beauty of the chilly December California morning.

Winter, lying on a blanket on the passenger seat, suddenly sits up and looks out the window. She knows we are near and I feel the urge to turn left at the next road. As I turn, the sunbeams start to light the green fields. There is a high grass area on the right and I slow down, knowing this is the place where we will find the dog in need. A large pipe runs under another abandoned farm acreage. There's an opening most dogs could go through. Is the dog stuck in there? Fortunately, the sun has come up enough so I can see clearly. Winter barks and I stop the car. Alex follows, parks, and gets out. There are no other cars, let alone people in view, only a ramshackle house and an uncared-for field with the big pipe nearby. I let Winter out and she walks toward the pipe like she knows her mission. As she heads for the pipe, Alex and I both know she is going inside it to find a dog.

Alex and I follow her. She speeds up to a good pace, and walks to the mouth of the pipe. She stops and barks once, then slowly enters the pipe.

Worried, I sit down on my knees in front of the pipe, not calling, but letting the dog know we are here. Alex stands by me. He sets a bowl of water down with the food and spreads down blankets by me.

It seems forever but it's only a few minutes until we hear movement deep in the pipe. Out comes Winter with a surprise. She's gently carrying a white newborn puppy in her mouth. Obviously, Buddy is not inside. But is there a mom in there with more puppies? The puppy looks only weeks old. Winter walks up and places the puppy carefully on my lap. Alex and I look at each other in disbelief. But Winter turns, going back into the pipe. I cradle the whimpering puppy in a blanket next to my chest. A few minutes later, Winter comes out with a second puppy, a black and white one this time. She carefully lays the puppy in my arms. Winter turns into the pipe again. The puppies begin to whimper louder for their mother. Are more puppies in there? My feeling is there are. Alex says, "She will be bringing the mother out next now." Lo and behold, Winter walks out with yet another white puppy, and following her is a very thin white pit bull mix with black spots. My heart drops. The mother looks so worn, and she is carrying a black and white puppy in her mouth. Winter carefully places the other puppy in my arms. Alex reaches his hand out to guide the mom to me. The mother follows his gesture and places her last pup in my arms. Somehow, she must know we are saving their lives. She slowly walks to the bowl to drink. She seems so thirsty. There must be very little water in the pipe. Where has she come from? How long have the poor dogs been in there? Then it comes to me in a vision, a moment. She was abandoned, dropped off while pregnant. How cruel some humans can be.

When the mother is finished drinking, Winter goes to her and stands close. In a low voice I say, "Come sweetie, you and your puppies are safe now." I probably don't need to talk because I'm sure Winter has communicated this to her. Alex helps me as I stand and we gather the puppies and slowly walk to my car. Winter walks beside the mom. Alex opens the back car door and Winter jumps in and I place the pups in my arms next to her. Alex places the next two in with the others. The mom just stands there so Alex takes a chance and says, "Come girl, you get in the car now with your little ones." He uses a gesture to show her the way. The mom looks at her pups, then him and tiredly gets in the car with the Alex's help. The puppies sidle up to their mom and begin nursing. I find tears are clouding my eyes. We place the food next to the mom and she takes a few bites but her eyes turn back to caring for her pups. Indeed, this poor mom is beyond exhausted. I get in the car and turn the engine on. Alex comes around to my side. I roll the window down and Alex and I discuss what to do. I text Jordana and he texts Andy's Rescue. He kisses me through the open window. "This is a miracle! I love you both. "

"Thank you. Love you too."

"Call me when you're finished at Andy's." We leave the area with our hearts full of sadness for the mistreatment of the mother but with bountiful joy that we found them. Through the miracle of a dream, we found the little family alive. The angels are near, for Winter's calling is that of a motherly comfort dog. She is definitely angel-sent. I'll have to ask Jerome again to tell me all he knows about her. Maybe there isn't anything else to tell. Andy will find homes for all the dogs; he and his wife have saved hundreds of dogs in the years since he started the rescue. But for now, the mom must gain strength and nurse her young.

The sun shines through the window and it's warm and snug for the mom and puppies in back by Winter's comfort. I call Jordana and we agree to meet at Andy's Rescue.

Andy and his wife, MJ are waiting for us as we pull up next to Jordana's car. MJ, Jordana, and I carefully take the pups. Andy picks up the mom. She seems to sense his kindness. Winter walks next to me, touching my jeans. We walk into the Rescue and the room where the little family will be cared for. Jordana takes over examining them all. Her healing hands seem to calm the mother as Jordana gives her an injection. Then mom is given food and she eats while lying down. A big dog bed is on the floor and when she's finished, we watch as she lies down. The pups are placed by her and begin nursing again.

Jordana says, "You found her in the nick of time. She is so very thin and dehydrated, and the puppies are so hungry."

Winter sits down by the mom and pups, their guardian on duty. I explain how we found them. "An angel sent Winter," Andy says. I don't look at Jordana, still so awed by the fact that she is an angel herself. Jordana agrees, "I believe it."

We stay awhile but I have to coax Winter to go home with me. I say my goodbyes and I tell them Winter and I will be back tomorrow morning to check on the dogs. Winter jumps in the front seat but looks longingly back at Andy's Rescue as I drive home. She is unlike any other dog I've ever known. I pet her head. "You did a good job today." I know in my heart she is attached to us. She has an ability to comfort, yet I see sorrow. I must need her more than she needs me. I will help her find her beloved human, if I can. But for now, we must try to find Buddy for Vince. I talk out loud to Dukie, "Is it really just a mere matter of time?"

Chapter 7

The Vision And Escape

Winter is happy to see the mom and pups the next morning when we arrive. Andy has fed the mother and she is nursing. MJ is at work and Andy will go later but the little home they've created for dogs is very comfortable. The rescues stay a limited time because Andy and MJ find homes quickly, mostly with people in town or friends of friends. Winter walks over and sits by the mom and her pups. The place is a safe haven until they're adopted, no matter how long it takes. Shining sunlight streams in the window like angel's light from above. Each dog has their own room with windows into the yard. There are plenty of blankets and pet beds and a doggy door access to the back yard. Andy and his wife have big hearts of gold, dedicating their lives to animals even though Andy runs the family hardware store and MJ works there too. Andy's mom is psychic as are many in town, and he's got a bit of the old vibe himself.

My meeting Andy in summer camp was a meant to be friends' moment. I was born in Mystic Bay but unfortunately my father died before I was born. My psychic mom and my adopted dad moved away to San Diego after my mom solved the April Sorenson case. People were wanting interviews then, standing outside our house and asking about our family to shopkeepers and neighbors in town since Mom was the psychic who solved the case. Because it was a missing child case, the headlines drew interest across the country. Of course, people scoffed at the idea that the child was fed berries by a big bear in a cabin, as the little girl said. She was very young, so they assumed April imagined it for comfort, like some children insist they have imaginary friends. But my mother visualized a Sasquatch nurturing her and so did Alex's late father. Someone nurtured her and kept her warm.

Unbeknownst to us until after we met, Alex's late father helped Mom with the case over thirty years ago. They were both psychic. He was on the force and was the first one to believe in her abilities to find the girl.

To get away from the notoriety, we moved to San Diego, but I spent every summer of my life with my aunt and uncle in Mystic Bay. I dreamed of moving back, and finally as an adult my wish came true. Interviewing two years ago, I got hired for the meteorologist job I'd hoped for. My parents had rented my childhood home out for years and I bought the house from them for a deal. My mother and father were delighted I could move back to the quaint stucco house with blue shutters, a block from the ocean. The best news of all, it's next door to Aunt Nancy and Uncle Dick.

Why Andy and I are dear friends is a story of how hearts of children can bond even at a young age. Years ago, at summer camp, Andy Walin, was bullied by other boys from the very first day because of his different mannerisms and atypical social ways. He had an unusual way of walking and eating and a few mean boys at the summer camp would imitate him, laughing. They teased him mercilessly, so other kids avoided Andy too. Nice kids are always afraid of bullies but somehow, I wasn't. He told me when we grew older, that he is on the Autism Spectrum and that's why kids teased him.

But when I met him at only nine, I saw the differences but knew he was a nice and funny boy who needed a friend. Andy and I became fast friends. Along with Maggie, we all bonded from our first day of summer camp. When we reminisced not long ago, Andy told me he'd always remember that he couldn't believe I wasn't afraid of the boys and how I stuck up for him. I remember it was at lunch time and they kept teasing him and calling him names as he ate his sandwich. I remember telling the bullies something like, "I don't think you guys are kings of the camp, so go away if you can't be nice to us kids!" I guess I was brave and they were afraid of little old me. They moved on to another table and never bothered him again. I'd stare them down when I saw them near him. It's funny when I think about it.

Andy said, "At lunch the first day, you'd motioned Maggie to come over and we sat with Mandy in her wheelchair. The bullies mocked her too, but you scared them away." He laughs at the thought. "We had fun and I felt so happy then. It took a while but the mean boys softened about Mandy and me although they stayed away because they were afraid of you. From that day forward, we slowly became accepted by all. If Mandy had grown into adulthood, she would express the same gratitude that I do. You know, today, you're still using that angel-given kindness, helping people and animals alike. Do you still stare bullies down?"

I laughed and said, "Haven't had to do that since, but I could if I needed to." I told him I appreciated the thought but that it was he and MJ, who are the protective angels of animals.

It's a wonderful way to live, I think, while watching Winter make the rounds to each puppy.

Laurjean popped in to see the mom and pups. We sat down and the mother seemed to love Laurjean instantly and Laurjean was overwhelmed by the story. With the puppies nursing their mom, kindhearted Laurjean teared up and she declared, "I want to adopt the mom and two pups. Donnie and I always help animals from Andy's Rescue and when he called us, well, I said I'd come right over. Our old Pitbull, Smokey, is getting on and our two pugs are gone so we need some liveliness. Smokey will be happy to have companions again. We've always had at least three dogs."

Laurjean thinks she'll name the mom Elfie, as she has pointed ears just like an elf. We are thrilled and before I leave with Winter, I tell her about my angel dream and how it has set me on a journey to find a man's stolen dog, and how it led me to these dogs. Laurjean is not surprised, "This town is full of psychics and angels on earth." She winks because Andy is with us and he doesn't know the secret. Alex and I guard her well-kept secret. Her gentle big husband, Donnie, is an angel living a human experience here too. Her son is a half-angel like Alex. Miracles in town, that's what they are.

"Laurjean, how's Gio doing?"

"He's just great, so helpful and nice. He can cook too. Thanks for finding him for us."

We decide we all need to get going, Laurjean to the restaurant and Andy to the hardware store. I take Winter home deciding to take Magic and Ralph for a short walk on the finest of December mornings. The sun is shining, not a cloud in the sky and I realize that even though today is a day off for me, I still need to search for Buddy on the Internet and make calls. Tomorrow, Saturday, I'll report the weather from Sommerset House and promote the shelter's Christmas fundraiser.

Before I go out, I text Vince's number telling him that I am still searching for Buddy. But Vince's text back surprisingly reads, "I don't think you will find Buddy. This guy I know says I can have his dog." My heart drops. That's all he writes.

I wait for a moment. I text. "Okay." He doesn't text back and a wave of disappointment washes over me. He's giving up that easily? Something is not right about this and then I remember Jerome said something about the other dogs Vince has found. Despite that, in my heart, my desire to find Buddy is even stronger than ever. Dukie was in my dream. He wants me to find Buddy. The last time my angel dream was true to her message and I did help solve a crime in the making, but with a twist. Will finding Buddy somehow have a twist of its own?

The short walk along to dog beach pathway is calming. I stop and let the dogs off the leash. Magic gallops around like a pony, while Winter and Ralph look on. Ralph stays close to me and sniffs the sand. But Winter just stands looking at the sea as if in soft reflection. Her brown eyes look up at me, her black furry face with the whitest eyebrows and muzzle makes me laugh. "Sweet Winter, what do you think in that bright mind of yours?" I lean over to pet both dogs. "Ralph, you are the best boy, I love you."

The sun is warm on my face but my eyes start feeling heavy. When I close them, the sunbeams seem to warm my soul. The soothing sound of the wave helps me silently pray for the angels to help me find Buddy. If Vince doesn't want him now, I will make sure he gets a home. I find myself falling asleep. I am fighting the sleepiness but suddenly a vision comes. I see my angel pointing to a woman kneeling, and crying, holding two brown dogs. She is praying, "Please send someone to help these dogs, please send me angels." The young woman is in a small mobile home. The vison ends and I open my eyes, staring at the sea.

I innately know I must help her, and right away. The angel has another mission for me and I'm gaining insight with rapid visions now like my mother before me. I look down at Winter and she is still gazing into my eyes. Winter knows what's happening. I'm sure of it. Has she seen my vision? We must go find these dogs, but how?

I sit for a moment on a bench. Magic jumps in my lap and I hold her close. Ralph and Winter sit dutifully gazing out at the vastness. The waves have a rhythm to them and passersby nod and wave. Fortunately, no one has come up to speak to me. I must concentrate. How will I help find where the woman and her dogs are located?

My angel whispers, *"Go. It will be alright."* Her whispering lingers in my mind for a moment and with new-found confidence I get up, leashing the dogs and walking slowly home, as Ralph can't walk briskly. Otherwise, I'd run. No time to call Alex until I'm in the car. Winter and I will go. I put Ralph and Magic in the house, pet them, and tell them I'll be back. Maurice is still napping on the window sill in the noonday sun. He opens one eye and shuts it again. Winter and I leave. We get it the car but where will I go? Alex is working hard on a case and I don't want to call him. Winter is in the passenger seat and we look at each other. "I don't know where we're going, Winter. Angel, please, show me the way."

I back out of the driveway and drive out of town, this time towards the north, sensing this is the way to go. Somehow the name of the town, Tardenville, enters my mind. It's the next town east of Hillsboro. How sad that a wealthy town like Hillsboro has an impoverished town so close to it. Why can't the people of Hillsboro help Tardenville folks, like our town helped Riverton become more prosperous years back? Riverton, the town southeast of us, is thriving now, especially since our town fundraised and built the Angel Museum there. Businesses have moved in and jobs are plentiful. It's becoming a charming town like Mystic Bay, and we call it our sister town.

Sighing, I calm down a bit because the afternoon sun has warmed the car and I feel certain that somehow, we will find the woman and her two dogs today. Driving on to Hillsboro, the cliffs are higher on Beach Road. I always marvel at how they rise up from the pewter sea toward heaven like praying hands.

Alex calls. He says, "Something is up, I know. Are you alright?" I tell him what's happened. "You can't go alone! I can't leave work yet, so I'm going to call Ken."

"I'll be fine. I'm not too far away now but I don't know the address. Maybe the dogs are sick. I think I can find them. You don't need to call Ken."

"I'm calling him. Don't forget he's an angel. He'll find you."

"I'll be fine. I'll call you when I find them." We hang up. How could Ken find me anyway? I know he's an angel but...I'm distracted. I concentrate, deciding to turn right towards the road to Tardenville. Minutes pass and I'm not sure what to do. I gain comfort from Winter. Now I know what it feels like to have her calming presence nearby. It was a beautiful thing to watch her being there calmed Elfie and her puppies. That's why Elfie knew it was okay to come out of the drain and for Winter to take her puppies from her. The thought of this miracle calms me. I see a sign that I'm entering Tardenville's main road. I stop the car for a moment to get my bearings. Turn right, I think, turn right. I drive a half mile and see a sign that reads, Tardenville Acres. Ahead are many old mobile homes close together. How will I find the young woman and the dogs? I slow down to a crawl, then stop again to think, closing my eyes. Suddenly, Winter jumps in the back. I turn to look back at her and when I turn around, I see Ken in the passenger seat next to me! Startled, I have the wits to compose myself. "Ken!"

He says softly, "I'm sorry Gayle, Alex called me that you needed help right away."

I catch my breath. My heart swells with thanksgiving. Here he is a real live angel yet he looks just like any ordinary big guy wearing a sweatshirt, jeans, and sneakers, something Alex would wear.

"Ken, thank you." I explain the vision, the woman and dogs needing help.

"Gayle, this is what we angels do. It's quite extraordinary; you had a daydream vision."

Alex calls again and I tell him Ken is with me and that we'll keep him informed. I turn to Ken, "I feel I have to drive down that road near the edge of the mobile park, the last street near a field."

"Go," he says

Slowly I drive along the few remaining streets. We turn down the last street. It looks just like I thought it would in my mind. Winter barks once, and a dilapidated home catches my eye. I tell Ken, "There are two dogs in there and I think we need to get the woman to safety too. They're in harm's way."

'Okay," Ken says. "There isn't a vehicle in front. I'll walk with you to the door."

"She's alone with the dogs. I'll leave Winter in the car. She'll calm the two dogs if we can take them."

I get out of the car with a racing heart and walk up the path and steps to the door. No one is around to watch us. Ken is a few feet behind me. A young, thin woman answers my knock. "Yes?" she says. Her eyes are red from crying and she looks so weary. Two medium-sized brown mixed dogs stand behind her. Neither of them looks like a German Shepherd, as Vince described Buddy. They are too small and look like they're from the same litter. Instinctively, I know they have sweet natures.

I use the softest voice I have. "I'm here to help you and your dogs. I know you want them to go to a safe place."

She looks stunned and says, "How did you know? I prayed for an angel."

"I was told to come here."

"Please," she says, "Take them before my boyfriend comes back. He said they have to be gone before he comes home from work or he'll get rid of them! I'm afraid he'll hurt them. He's on his way, coming home soon."

"We need to move fast," I tell her. I take a chance and say the words I think she needs at this very moment: "Would you like to come with us? I know a place you'll be safe too. It's in Mystic Bay."

She seems surprised but says, "Yes. Can you pick up Bobbi and I'll take Lulu." She grabs a purse and jacket and picks up the one called Lulu. I pick up the thinner one, Bobbi. They are both straggly looking, but seem to know that we are taking them to safety. As we walk, I say, "My friend is here to help us."

The young woman says, "The dog in the car will help us?" I look at Ken as he walks with us realizing the woman can't see him. Then, I hear his voice in my mind. "*I didn't want to frighten her.*" Stunned, I not only hear Ken telepathically but see him. I remain composed as Winter is looking out the side window. I open the car door. "My dog's name is Winter and she is a friend to all dogs. She's a comfort dog."

The woman and I place the two dogs in with Winter. There are blankets and Winter sniffs the two of them and they cuddle up next to her. I shut the door. Instantly, Ken is in the back seat with them. I don't react. It's unbelievable yet real. The two sweet-faced dogs look at him with love knowing I'm sure that he's an angel. The woman and I get in the car but the miracle of it all stops me from starting the car or speaking for a moment. The dogs can see Ken, the angel, like all dogs can.

Composing myself, driving away, I tell the woman I will take her to a shelter and then the dogs to a friend's animal shelter. "Maybe you can be reunited."

"They're not my dogs," she tells me. "I found them wandering around the trailer park yesterday. I knocked on doors but no one claimed them so I took them in and made hamburgers for them. My boyfriend was angry and it was a rough night. I told him I'd find a place for them today but I don't have a car." She starts to cry and her phone beeps. "It's him texting me. He's entering the park! He says the dogs better be gone."

Immediately in protection mode. I tell her, "Put your head down so he doesn't see you." She quickly does as told. Little sparkles of light come over the back seat toward the woman ducking down. What is he doing? Amazing to me, I realize Ken is sending her crystal angel dust. They are just like those sparkles that came over me at the shelter. They remind me of a calming breeze and I feel calm as I drive toward the entrance. A dirty yellow truck buzzes by with an angry looking man driving. He doesn't look at me. Good. I wait a few seconds before I say, "He just passed by us."

She sits up and looks back behind us. She looks at the dogs but of course can't see Ken. She turns back to me. "Did an angel send you?"

"Yes, I had a vision to come get you and the dogs. It happens to me sometimes. What's your name?"

"Dalia."

"I'm Gayle. Everything will work out, don't worry." Dalia's phone rings. "It's him," she says trembling.

"It's okay. Don't answer it. Turn your phone off until we get to the shelter and they will know how to handle it." I wait as she turns her phone off then I say, "It's a woman's shelter called July's Place and was started by July North, the talk show host. It's a wonderful place. I'll call my friend Maggie who volunteers there. Maybe she can meet you there."

"Okay, thank you." Dalia looks in the back seat again, obviously not seeing Ken. "Will they find homes for them?"

"Yes, don't you worry. We will find them happy homes."

"Together please. They love each other."

"Absolutely, Dalia. We will make sure of it."

I call Maggie's cell and she answers. "Maggie, can you meet me at July's Place in a half hour? I have a woman named Dalia in my car and she needs help." Maggie doesn't hesitate or ask me the circumstance, knowing I have a situation and need her. She tells me she will meet us there. I hang up and realize Dalia seems a bit calmer now as more angel dust floats around her from Ken. She closes her eyes as I drive, and this is good. I would never have believed when I woke up this morning that I would be on a mission to help Dalia and the dogs.

I drive a few minutes and she says, "I've only got sixty dollars to my name."

"Don't worry, the staff will help you there. We've a way to go. I'll let you know when we're nearing Mystic Bay." Dalia asks about July's Place. "It's a wonderful shelter and you can stay as long as you need to. They'll help you with a place to live, and schooling if you need it for a job. The dogs will go to Andy's Rescue. He's my friend and he'll find the dogs a good home. I'm going to call Andy now."

Andy is at work but will go home to meet us. After the call ends and we drive miles away from Tardenville, Dalia lays her head back and closes her eyes again. I know Ken is in the back and knowing he's been here all along comforts me too. No sound from the dogs but I'm sure they are sleeping. The sun is shining brightly at nearly two o'clock as we drive down Main Street turning on to the road for July's Place. Maggie and I look like sisters, everyone says, and true to her nature she is standing waiting in front of the homey clapboard house. It has a welcoming feel, the typical vibe of Mystic Bay with Christmas wreaths on every window. Outside the house, a plastic snowman stands with a black hat and a carrot nose. He greets us as if he's waiting for us, a welcoming presence for Dalia. I take my seat belt off before opening the car door, and Dalia puts her hand on my arm. "I prayed all night for help. Are you an angel? "

"No, Dalia, but an angel did send me. Angels are near Dalia, nearer than you could ever imagine."

"Thank you."

"Dalia, it's you who are these dogs' angel." She smiles. We get out of the car and Maggie introduces herself and Dalia stops and leans in to talk to the dogs but Ken isn't there. He's disappeared in the afternoon light. "Goodbye Lulu and Bobbi. I love you. Find someone good enough to give you a home."

"I'll make sure they stay together. I promise."

I hug her and Maggie hugs her too. I wonder if Maggie saw Ken disappearing but her knowing look tells me she did. She sees angels as her great grandmother did before her. She links her arm in Dalia's and they walk up the steps to the house where a new start waits for Dalia. I turn to look at the dogs before driving off. Winter's warmth snuggles them to her. I drive on to Andy's Rescue, teary but knowing Lulu and Bobbi will find a home. Andy, my incredible childhood friend will see to it. It's the way in Mystic Bay, a peaceful, friendly way to live, helping those in need. It must be the sea air bringing the angels nearby.

Chapter 8
Andy's Rescue

Andy is waiting and helps me get the dogs out of the car, carrying Lulu as I carry Bobbi to their temporary home. Winter comes along, walking as close to me as possible. Andy has made a comfortable kennel for them with beds, blankets, food, and water, just like Elfie's room. "Jordana will come over soon and check them over." Andy bends to pet dear Winter. "Good girl."

"Shall we stay awhile to help?"

"Why don't you visit Elfie and her pups for a little while. They're doing so well. I'll tend to these two."

Winter and I walk into the room that houses Elfie and her puppies. Winter's tale wags at almost hummingbird speed and when Elfie looks at me for a moment, I see happiness in her eyes. My ability to see their souls is increasing. It's humbling to know I can sense their emotions. We stay for a while and then I call Winter to go with me, but she doesn't budge. Andy comes in to talk to us and I tell him, "Winter wants to stay with them today. Will that be alright? She knows her mission is to comfort them." Andy says, "Of course, she can help me."

"Do you need me to stay, Andy?"

"No, thanks. You go home. You've rescued all these dogs in two days, and I'm amazed at what you can do. I wonder what their story is. I sense their sadness, as I'm sure you do."

"It's a pity that some humans don't have a soulful connection to animals and treat them so poorly. You're doing a wonderful thing.

Maybe Alex and I can take them and make them ours. What's two more dogs? Just more to love."

"I was thinking the same thing. MJ and I have two but these two dogs seemed to immediately bond with me."

"Remember you're both angels on earth, Andy."

"Thank you, I feel the same about you two. Now you go home. I'll put Miss Winter here to work snuggling all the dogs."

"Okay, Alex will pick her up. He'll be here about seven, is that okay?"

"Sure is. Winter is a real gem of a comfort dog."

I kneel down to hug Winter. "Alex will pick you up, Winter." Her eyes look happy. She seems to understand. "Andy, I'd like to bring Winter here with me to volunteer on days you might need us. I work on the weekends and some hours during the week but most week days are good for me."

"Terrific. Thank you! We'll be happy to have you and Winter."

Reluctantly, I say goodbye and leave driving the short distance home again contemplating Winter's personality, so very different from other dogs I've had or known. But still, I worry. She loves the dogs and sits with Alex in his big, red recliner as he speaks softly to her, but at night, she waits by the fireplace looking at the front door. She won't sit on the couch. *"Give her time,"* the words flow through my mind from the angels.

When I call Alex, he tells me not to worry about Winter because it hasn't been a week since she came home with me and we've rescued two sets of dogs in that time. "She's been on the streets, so maybe this is all foreign to her, never having had a real home, a blanket, or a bed." I know he's right but I will try to find the person she was with, if possible. Jerome said he just found her that day outside the shelter and no one knew where she came from. I'll look for the answers. Maybe I'll even find Buddy. It doesn't matter that Vince doesn't want Buddy back now. I'm determined to find the dog.

At home, I prepare a Cobb salad dinner. I call Maggie to say thank you before she has her own dinner.

"Everything has gone well, Gayle. Dalia's in her own room and I left just a little while ago. You did a great thing today. The angels sent you on a special journey. Who knows what's next."

"Thank you. How are you feeling?"

"Well, I'm feeling pretty good now. Tomorrow, we find out the gender of our baby. Of course, I know it's a girl. You do too, don't you?"

"I do. I'm seeing a beautiful face, a combination of yours and Noah's. She'll look a lot like Marshall."

"I agree."

I tell her about Winter's maternal instincts and how she seems attached to us but there is a loneliness about her, like she's waiting for her old companion.

Maggie is silent for a while but her psychic vibe comes through. "Yes, she's wondering where he is, I feel. But all will work out." We hang up the phone and I feel fortunate to have a close friend like her. She sees things intuitively too. But these visions are really happening to me more quickly, and to Alex with his own incredible gift of intuition. It's escalating for both of us again like it did when we worked on the Parker case.

When Alex walks in the kitchen with Winter, I kneel down to hug her. The other animals run to her. Yes, love has expanded in our household to include Winter. We love our special, mothering comfort dog. "Sweet Winter," I tell her. I see a smile in her eyes yet a longing too. In my mind I tell her, "I'll find him Winter. I'll try."

Chapter 9

A Change In The Christmas Air

I wake up without a dog rescue dream. Alex has told me not to worry. "Just think positive thoughts today." But I can't help but fret. I am on my way to Sommerset House. I put on my Christmas sweatshirt and earrings again then say goodbye to my animal companions, kiss my husband, and get into my car with a latte to go. Alex and I bought our favorite, a machine that can make espresso for him and latte for me.

On the way home, I'll have to stop by the Heaven Can't Wait store and thank Ken. His help yesterday with the rescue of Bobbi and Lulu and, of course, getting Dalia to safety, gave me even more courage to search for Buddy. I also will invite Gio for a spaghetti dinner with Maggie, Noah, and baby Marshall tonight, and I'll include Andy and MJ. Maggie will reveal the baby's gender to us although we both intuitively know it's a girl.

It's beautiful out although cold at forty-nine degrees, but the mist is light as I head into San Francisco. I won't have time to look for Buddy today but maybe I'll get a vision. Just maybe, I pray.

At Sommerset House, volunteers are wrapping gifts and labeling donated items. Tyler Parker is there and I'll interview him before I relay today's unbelievably gorgeous forecast of a sunny day. Tyler takes Saul and me to the apartments that families and singles are moving into today and the rest of December. One and two-bedroom apartments with living areas are almost complete. We marvel at the furniture, both new and donated, and the kitchens with everything a family or single person would need. Nice windows to look out of, but mostly a place to call home.

Taking the TV viewers on the tour, Chase is very upbeat, asking me about the apartments and I tell him how people will love living here. Tyler states that Christmas at Bay Star will be the best ever for many in San Francisco. We end our interview and head for the station, as Wes wants to see me. Sunday, I'll bring Magic with me to Sommerset House. It's great to think I won't have to be in the studio with Mitzy again until after Christmas. I say my goodbyes, thrilled with the progress Tyler is making.

I arrive at work and before I go into Wes's office, I stop by the ladies' room. Of course, as is my luck, Mitzy walks in. "Oh, you're here?"

"I've a meeting with Wes."

I am polite as usual but of course I can tell she's gearing up to say something about my sweatshirt and dangly Christmas bangle earrings. Why can't I stand up to her like I did years ago to those bullies who were mean to Andy? I know why. I've matured and know the best way to handle her.

Here she goes. I'm not surprised when she says, "Santa Claus is coming to town early this year. Look at you, so... well Christmas personified. Are you wearing Springtime in Paris perfume? It always smells like my grandma when I visited her in the nursing home."

I wait a beat then say in the sweetest way," Why Mitzy, the perfume reminds me of my dear grandma too. She loved this scent and you know what? It's my fave too. Thank you for reminding me of Grandma!" I walk out not turning back to see her or hear her reaction. Yikes, she's something. But I was polite, thankfully. I sniff my wrists before I walk into Wes' office. I do love that perfume. As I walk into the office, Wes greets me with the biggest smile. "You did a great job today, Gayle."

"Thanks Wes."

"Listen, please sit down for a moment. I want to ask you something important." I sit and smile, wondering what this could be about? His face changes. I intuitively know it's about Mitzy. "I've had complaints about Mitzy and well, I wonder if you have had problems with her."

Not shocked I say, "She does a very good job doing the traffic."

"Gayle, as usual, you are so polite," Wes says with one eyebrow raised. "You must have had an incident or two. Everyone has."

"She's made a few comments. I don't throw anyone under the bus, Wes." My stomach has a knot in it.

"Look, you are our own Miss Congeniality and I appreciate how you get along with everyone but I need your help."

Uh oh, I think. What's he going to say?

"Would you be willing to mentor Mitzy, counseling her on how to get along better with her coworkers?"

I don't reply. He waits a moment, then adds, "Do it for me, please. You're the only one who could do it. Your bit of intuition could help her. You may even save her from being fired."

My angel on my shoulder of course prompts me to say, "Yes, I'll do it, but only if she asks me herself."

"Thank you, thank you," Wes says, getting up to let me know our conversation is over.

"Her dad and I know each other and he's frustrated with her work record. I really appreciate it. She asked for you herself, as I've had a talk with her already this morning."

We shake hands and I leave the station wondering why I'm so eager to please, but it's okay. I sigh. She asked for me? She probably won't like the thought of me mentoring her, really. Then a thought comes to me that there is a lot I don't know about her. Maybe something stands in her way of being friendly?

I'm tired as I drive back to Mystic Bay but the open road brings me peace, knowing all the animals we found are safe with Andy and our animals are waiting for me at home. Alex will be preparing the house for company.

Driving down Main Street the homespun decorations in town fill my heart with the Christmas spirit. Every building is bedecked with hanging baskets with pine and poinsettias in them. People are walking down Main Street chatting happily, carrying packages and there is Christmas in the California air even without snow. I stop at Heaven Can't Wait, Ken's angel store. The store is filled with all sizes and kinds of artificial trees with angel ornaments and more. Gifts are everywhere in the room. A few customers are walking around, and I see Ken wrapping a gift at the counter. I wave. "Hi Gayle." His glow and smile are spun with gold.

"Ken, I just came in to thank you for helping me with everything." I try to keep my voice soft so the customers can't overhear.

"You're welcome. It's a beautiful day, isn't it?"

"Yes, it is. Tonight, we're having a few friends over for my unfamous spaghetti. I invited Gio, Andy and MJ, and Maggie and Noah. You and your family are invited as well."

"We'd love to, Gayle, but Saturday is our family night. We're taking the kids over to their Aunt Mabel's. Thank you, though. Maybe another time?"

"Well, as a matter of fact, on Christmas Eve we're going to start an annual trim-the-tree open house for anyone who wants to drop by, starting at three. Everyone can put an ornament on the tree, if they choose, and we're serving simple fare, sandwiches and goodies made by my aunt. I know it's family time but I thought I'd invite you all to stop by"

"Well, that's so nice. We'll be there for a little while for sure. By the way, anything new happening with Buddy?"

I explain how Vince is not interested in Buddy anymore and he plans to get another dog. "I'm still going to find him somehow; I feel it my heart."

"You follow your heart, and if you need me, you call me or have Alex call me."

"Thanks Ken!" I marvel at the fact that I'm talking to a real angel living a human life and we're actually friends. I've seen him fly with his glorious wings. I've seen his heavenly abilities helping people and animals in need. We hug goodbye but then he stops me. "Here, please, take this for your tree, because the angels tell me you will find Buddy." It's a small dog ornament, a German Shepherd, gold and black with angel wings."

"Oh Ken, I love it, it looks like Buddy might look. Thank you so much!"

"You are so welcome, Gayle. Now go, have a good day and some good dreams too."

Smiling, we say goodbye and I leave clutching the little dog ornament to me. I will find Buddy because Ken's an angel and the angels know.

On my way and almost home, I get a call from an unknown number, so as usual I don't want to answer it, but then I get the vibe it's Mitzy. Oh, I wish I didn't have to answer but of course I do. "Hello, this is Gayle."

"Uh Gayle, it's Mitzy Blane. Wes said he talked to you this morning about my predicament."

"Yes, he did." I wait for her to ask me as I'm not going to offer to help unless she has the wherewithal to ask.

"Would you be my mentor?" She doesn't say please but I will do it because she called and asked.

"Yes, of course, Mitzy. I was thinking if you called, we could meet Monday on both our days off at a coffee house I know near the station."

"Oh, could you come to Hillsboro where I live? There's a coffee shop in Pal's Captain's Inn near my condo."

"Okay. How about ten on Monday." Mitzy is still pushy. I suddenly feel there is something she's keeping from me. She's on an improvement plan and I'm responsible for helping. Ugh.

"I won't see you tomorrow because I'll be at Sommerset House again doing interviews, but if you need to talk to me for any reason just text, okay?"

"Okay." Then we hang up and I wonder how I will approach the subject with her. I guess, like always, I will try to be soft, composed and kind. It's all I know. Then I laugh to myself about those bullies years ago and how I got the situation to turn around.

Chapter 10
Spaghetti With Friends

G io arrives first with red carnations for me. How sweet of him. He looks good and is happy with his jobs and the people he works with. He's very cordial when meeting Alex and kneels down to greet all our animal companions. He talks to each one and seems to love holding Maurice. Maurice does not cotton to everyone. "I love cats too," he states. I tell him, "Gus texted me he's coming the twenty-third. You must be excited. He sounds great."

"I can't wait. You know everyone is so nice here. I feel at home already. Ken and Jamie are helping me fix up the apartment, so when Gus comes, we can sign the papers and stay there that night."

"That's really great, Gio." His speech is more relaxed and confident. It's good to see the change.

Maggie and Noah arrive next with Marshall who walks up to the dogs. The dogs love the little toddler. Maurice, however, runs under Alex's red chair. He does not like the attention or lots of people in the house. Gio's voice is stronger now as he meets our friends. We start sitting down at the big table to my spaghetti, salad, and garlic bread. Andy and MJ arrive and introductions are made. I don't make my own sauce but I do doctor it up the way Mom and Grandma did, with a little garlic, onion, wine and more. Everyone is busy twirling their spaghetti and I smile, watching Andy begin eating his garlic bread, turning it round and round like he always does. It reminds me of how squirrels eat their nuts. This is what those bullies laughed at while he ate his peanut butter and jelly at camp. Andy notices me looking at him and must have read my mind or have seen Gio look at him with a quizzical look, for he winks at us. We laugh, but I'm sure Gio doesn't know why we're laughing. We are all different in many ways, aren't we?

With glasses raised, Alex proposes a toast, "To you, our guests. Christmas Eve we will have our first annual Christmas trim-the-tree open house and you are all invited for libations, food, and to help us put an ornament or two on our tree. We are inviting our favorite people to stop by on the way to family parties or stay if you have no other plans. We're starting at three! "

Every one of them say they want to join us. Then Maggie and Noah share their news their new baby girl is on the way and they have chosen a name. Maggie says, "I had a dream the night after we knew we were having a girl. Mandy, my late childhood friend, meant a lot to me, as Gayle and Andy know. She suffered from cerebral palsy. But in my dream, she was grown up, and in heaven was perfect physically. She spoke to me. She told me how she loved me and appreciated the three of us and our friendship way back then. Then she was gone, and I woke up. I told Marshall that morning, "We are going to have a baby sister for you. Her name will be Mandy Gayle. And Marshall said to me, 'She colors rainbows now.' Hearing that, I was overwhelmed with the beauty of the thought. Mandy Gayle painting rainbows. Sorry Andy, we tried to fit your name in somewhere. But would you be her godfather?"

"You bet; I'd be honored!"

Alex and I hug them both. Everyone congratulates them and I can hardly eat, I feel so over-the-top happy.

"How special is this?" Alex toasts again and we all talk of angels and the miracles in Mystic Bay. Gio is captivated by all the angel tales. I watch him listening again to the stories of the three children who saw angels a few years back. He's in awe when Maggie tells him how her late great grandmother, Madam Norma, saw angels all the time and helped counsel others with guidance from the angels. We speak of Noah's new book just out, "They Believe They Saw Angels," which recounts real stories of townsfolk and others. He wants to give us all the book this Christmas. Gio is thrilled. I remember Gio has his own loving story of his late grandmother coming to his bedside. The last bit of the apple pie is finished, and we talk about the two dog rescues this week, so Gio tells Andy and MJ, "Anytime you need someone to help, I would like to help volunteer, if I'm not working."

Andy and MJ are delighted.

Gio is last to leave. "When Noah brings you his book, please tell him the story of your Grandma Maria. Maggie tells me he is writing another edition to this book with more accounts of angels."

Gio says he will. "Thank you both for a lovely time. You make me feel so welcome."

"This is your home now," Alex says.

"Sleep well, Gio," I say giving him a hug. We watch him as he walks on down our street toward Main Street where his new apartment awaits.

Yes, it was a good spaghetti night with old friends, and a new friend too. With everyone gone and the kitchen cleaned, Maurice comes out from under the red recliner so we take the animals outside to the cold night sky.

Alex says, with his arm around my shoulders, "What do you think next week's miracles will be?"

"Vince's interest in finding Buddy is gone, but my determination has strengthened. I will find the dog. I have asked the angels to help me and they will."

"I'm sure of it."

I tell him about Wes asking me to help Mitzy and what's transpired. "She's not into it."

Alex ponders and then his intuition kicks in. "I'm afraid, Gayle, that I sense heartache, do you? Something sad in her life."

"Maybe, but what could cause such rudeness?"

"Time will tell us." Hand-in-hand we walk back in the house, heading for our night's sleep with little Magic, old Ralph and Maurice trailing behind us into the bedroom. But even though this week with Winter has been one of rescuing and comforting the dogs and apparently becoming attached to us, she walks back to her bed by the fireplace. "It's okay," I tell her, petting her head. "Sleep well, my beautiful soul. Dream all things good and may your loved one be near." But as I go to my bed, I wonder. Will I be able to let her go if Jerome or I find her favorite person, a man? Yes, I'm sure it was a man.

Chapter 11
The Synchronicities

It's Monday, I'm meeting Mitzy at The Coffee Nook at Pal's Captain's Inn in Hillsboro. But this morning, I drop Winter off at Andy's Rescue. She will stay all day with Elfie and her pups. Miraculously, MJ and Andy have decided to keep Bobbi and Lulu for their own. Now they'll have four dogs but they are thrilled. I will tell Maggie to pass the news to Dalia. Maggie says she's doing well and she's invited her to the annual Christmas Day parade.

Mitzy is late so I sit in a booth, having ordered my latte at the counter. The restaurant and Inn are so picturesque and even the coffee place has windows looking out to the sea. I realize I'm nervous because my intuition tells me Mitzy's heart isn't in this mentoring thing. I wonder if she'll critique my red sweater with silver reindeer and, of course, the matching reindeer studs in my ears. My hair is down as it usually is when out and about, with little makeup so I won't get recognized. Mitzy finally walks in. She really is stunning looking with dark hair flowing and her makeup sheer perfection, dressed in a white pantsuit, red heels, and red wool scarf. "Hello Mitzy," I say standing. "Glad to see you." She only smiles and sits down. She has her own coffee from Stars Coffee. Uh oh, I doubt that the management here will approve but I don't say anything about bringing in drinks from somewhere else. "You look so nice. What a beautiful pantsuit."

"You, well, you really shouldn't wear that sweater and earrings, Gayle. It's something fifty-year old's wear. "

I sigh and begin. "Mitzy, it's rude to criticize others clothes or anything they're wearing unless they ask you your opinion. To be blunt, I would have asked you to be honest about my clothing choice today if I wanted your advice. If I did ask you, you could have said you thought plain colors look better on me or something like that. Do you want to role play what to say and what not to say to someone?"

"No, this is stupid. I can't help being honest. It's just you are a beautiful woman and really you do look much better without that TV makeup and some of the older lady clothes and colors you wear. That green Christmas sweatshirt has to go."

"That is the sweatshirt for the fundraiser for Bay Star Shelter but I have to say thank you for saying I look beautiful." I smile but she doesn't. She is so frustrating. I take a sip thinking about what to say next, when unbelievably my old sort-of-boyfriend, Detective Beau Bolton, walks in the Coffee Nook. He and I had a brief romance and I do mean brief, but he really was helpful solving the Parker case with me and Alex last year. Of course, Detective Bolton sees me and comes over. He's a very good-looking man and of course I notice Mitzy looking him up and down. "Gayle, wow, it's great seeing you, it's been way too long."

"Hey, Beau," I smile. "This is my coworker, Mitzy Blane." I can't say she's my friend because she's not.

"Well, hello," he smiles that smile that breaks so many hearts. Mitzy's negative demeanor with me is off-putting, but she is beautiful.

"Hello there," she says as she flutters her fake lashes.

He turns to me again, "How's Alex?"

"He's good, thanks." I don't ask him to sit down but I'm sure Mitzy would like that."

"Well, if you find more cases to solve with your psychic ways that need my expertise just give me a call." He tells Mitzy it was nice meeting her and goes to get a coffee.

"Wow, he's gorgeous," Mitzy whispers loudly, practically foaming at the mouth. I'm sure Beau heard her. "What case were you on?"

It's then an angel in my mind tells me she knows; she knows all about my case. I guess it's just the scuttlebutt around the coffee at work. "Oh, I'm sure you've heard about it." I change the subject.

"So how would you like to proceed? Do you want to discuss how to change dynamics with some of your relationships at work?"

"Not really. Wes says I just needed a couple of pointers and you gave me some. Don't tell people how you feel about their clothing until you're asked. See? I'd rather talk about that case you were on. I'm interested in detective work. I've heard you're famous for putting a guy in jail."

"Not famous at all." I want to say that I'm positive Wes didn't tell her she needed one statement from me on how to have good work relationships. That's why I was asked to help her.

"Are you going to tell me about the case or not?"

"No, we're here to talk about you. Tell me about you. How do you like working at KHBW?"

Mitzy is clearly upset I'm not discussing the case. Beau walks by with his coffee and stops at our table. "Ladies," he says. Then I can't believe Mitzy has the nerve to say, "Why don't you join us? We're just chatting about that case you two were on. Are you a detective?"

Beau sits pulling up another chair. "Yes, a San Francisco Police detective. Gayle was the force to be reckoned with and no pun intended. She used her psychic abilities and solved a crime in the making along with the help of her husband, an amateur detective of sorts, and me, of course."

Mitzy puts her hand on Beau's arm, "She's psychic. That's what they say at the office. I heard Chase say Gayle that you can predict the weather too?" They both laugh at that joke and Beau continues while I fume. He looks at me, noting my expression. He says, "Gayle is too humble to explain." I can't tell him not to talk about it but of course he loves the limelight and begins.

"Well, you see Mitzy, Gayle is not only a meteorologist but one hell of a detective. She had an inkling to save an old man from harm."

"Really," Mitzy says with a flirtatious voice and smile. She can't take her eyes off him.

"Yeah, and she chose the other detective, her husband, over me. He was the luckier of the two of us."

Mitzy didn't like that one bit. "Really, how foolish to lose a good-looking man like you."

I feel ill. This counselling is going nowhere.

"How about you and I go out for a drink one night, Mitzy. I'll tell you the whole story of how Gayle solved the crime with her intuition. As a matter of fact, I saw you the other day, Gayle, interviewing Tyler Parker. He's thrilled his father is still alive because of you and now it looks like Tyler's giving back to the homeless community."

Mitzy asks, "Tyler Parker, the guy you're interviewing about the shelter?"

I decide to take the higher road, "Yes, that's who he is. Beau was a big part in solving the case and I will be forever grateful."

"This is so intriguing. I need to know more."

"Well, Mitzy," the savvy Beau flirts, "I'm available to have a drink, are you?"

"Why, yes I am." She looks at me surprised as I get up.

I say, "Well, while you two get acquainted, I've got to run, so sorry, but I'll see you at work Mitzy. It was nice seeing you again, Beau."

I smile while saying goodbye again and leave, wishing I had my heels on to click, click away. But instead, I wore my red reindeer flats so I walk away softly like a reindeer on snow. I bet Mitzy will tell me soon that my shoes looked like grandma slippers.

My mind has to leave her and turn to finding Buddy, and where my angel connection will lead me. I'm not going to continue trying to counsel Mitzy but will tell Wes that it's best to find someone else. There's something annoying about her, and she's quite intrusive besides rude. Why should she care about the case? It's weird and annoying. And Beau? A blast from the past. A romance that was brief yet he did help Alex with solving the case. It seems like that whole part of my life happened to someone else.

Driving back to Mystic Bay, I find solace looking at the ocean. Stop ruminating on the past and on Mitzy and Beau's behavior, I tell myself. When I pick up Winter, Andy tells me she's done rounds with the dogs, sitting for a while with Elfie and her pups then going into Bobbi and Lulu's space and walking outside with them. "They all love her like she's, their mama." Andy is thrilled telling me, "We're taking Bobbi and Lulu into our house this afternoon. They need to get to know our dogs but I know it will be fine."

"I happy for you both, and for the dogs." We say our goodbyes and Andy bends down to tell Winter, "Good job!" When we set off for home, I tell her she's a sweet girl. Her eyes look at me, such knowing eyes.

At home with the rest of my animal family, I change into my sweats to take the dogs for a short walk to Dog Beach. Magic is jumping on her hind legs as I find the leashes. Maurice yawns and rubs his body against me as if to let me know he's here. I've forgotten my knit cap and so I go into my closet looking for it. I feel an overwhelming sense of loss. What is it? Going into the bedroom, I open my drawer to get my gloves, then an urge comes over me to find the photo of my first dog, Dukie. I find the album with pictures of all the dogs I had as a child and as an adult. Looking at Dukie's sweet face in my favorite photo of him, I know dreaming of him and the dog that must be Buddy is really a calling. I remember Vince describing Buddy looking similar to Dukie. "Help me Dukie, show me the way."

The next few days go by without message dreams from my angel even though I ask every night. I report from Sommerset House on the progress made getting gifts for the kids, items for the new apartments, and A Christmas of Hope celebration. It's Friday and I stop in at the station to talk to Wes personally. Mitzy will be there tomorrow, and I've had to think long and hard about counselling her. Should I back down? I practice sitting in front of Wes to plead my case. "She just wasn't into it, Wes. I'm not a therapist." Then I question the whole thing. What if it is part of my angel connection to help Mitzy? No coincidence here; my phone rings and it's Mitzy.

"Hey, can we meet Monday in Mystic Bay at a restaurant? I want to see that town you live in."

To me this is ripe with irony, and actually funny. She's calling me to meet? "Sure, Mitzy same time?"

"Yes. Hey you walked out fast the other day and so if I was, well, offensive then I'm sorry."

Surprised that she sounds sincere, I reply, "Yes, you said you didn't want to talk about work with me."

"Well, I didn't but after that creep Beau stood me up for a date with a late text, I decided you must have a lot of good advice. I haven't ever been dumped by a text."

"Oh, it happens," I laugh. "He did you a favor. I'm looking forward to our meeting. I'll be at Sommerset House reporting the weather again tomorrow and Sunday so I'll see you Monday at nine this time, if that's good at The Next Door Café in Mystic Bay."

Mitzy actually thanks me and I end the call baffled but happy. I'm glad I didn't bother Wes. But as the synchrony of events keeps rolling on, Wes calls me.

"Hey, Wes."

"Hi. Mitzy called a few minutes ago and I'm so happy the mentoring is going well, Gayle. Mitzy came in this morning, and said you're doing a remarkable job and she's trying hard. She said she met one of your friends and learned all about the abilities you used to solve the Parker case. She's really quite in awe of your skills."

I'm taken aback. "Really?"

"Gayle, I didn't get one complaint when she filled in doing traffic this week."

Wes changes the subject and we discuss the Christmas Day event and Saul and the times I will be at the shelter. "I'm bringing Magic to Sommerset House tomorrow to report the weather."

"That's great, I'm glad," he responds. We hang up and I feel sort of okay that I'm continuing with Mitzy but remember I'm no counsellor, just a meteorologist, with a slight psychic ability. But the upcoming weather report looks good for Mitzy to keep her job at least for now.

When I arrive home, we have another good night eating pizza by the fire and dog and cat cuddling. Alex is happy for me and glad Mitzy is doing better. He has an idea and I really like it. He wants to meet Mitzy someday soon. He wants to see what he can discern with his intuition. "I feel she's troubled. Something hurtful happened to her. That's where her rude, defensive behavior comes from. Perhaps you should ask her about it." I agree with him. I look over at Winter and notice she is looking at me. The other animals are sleeping and Alex has closed his eyes too. On this Friday night, I get a thought in my mind from the angels. "*Winter knows you and Alex love her.*" If my heart could smile it would. My thoughts turn to Buddy. I will dream of him very soon. I know Dukie and the angels will show me where to find him.

Chapter 12
Monday And Mitzy

I'm sitting in the booth as Mitzy floats in. All eyes turn to see her beauty walk by. Dressed impeccably she wears all black designer pants, a sweater, and a coat with black boots. Her red, green, and black scarf is twirled ever so perfectly around her. Her hair is long and glistening. But something seems off.

"Hello Mitzy," I smile.

"Sorry, I'm late," she says. Laurjean comes round with her coffee pot, green streak in her blonde hair and completely dressed as an elf from the movie of the same name. She looks hysterically funny and I say, "Laurjean, you amaze me with your creativity." Mitzy looks her up and down in horror, mouth agape. "This is my coworker, Mitzy."

"Glad to meet you, Gio will take your order, gals." She sashays away and Mitzy watches and says, "You've got to be kidding? Creative, she isn't."

"She loves to dress up, Mitzy. It's the way she likes to have fun with the customers. That's something I learned a long time ago. Let people be whoever they want to be. She's a charming, kind woman and that's what really matters."

Mitzy sighs looking at the menu. Then she looks at me. "Wes said you are like Miss Congeniality. Don't you ever get tired of it?"

Suddenly, I laugh at this whole scenario. "No, I don't get tired. I'm just me."

Gio comes over to take our order and once again Mitzy is intrigued by another handsome though younger guy.

"Hi Gayle," Gio smiles and his voice level is perfectly normal. I introduce Mitzy to him. After we order she says, "You kind of look Italian like me, and remind me of that young actor what's his name, in the movie, *The Italian Connection*." She looks at me and I tell her I don't know the film. Gio seems embarrassed. "Yes, I'm Italian. Thanks, I guess."

"Are you from Chicago?"

"No, Iowa." He leaves after taking our order of Sunshine Pancakes.

"Do you know anyone single but not that young? After Beau's text, I'm getting paranoid."

"Don't be, Mitzy. It's his M. O. Love 'em and leave 'em. He only wanted to see me again after I started dating Alex."

"Oh," she seems befuddled for a moment then changes the subject.

"I want you to know I worked a few days this week and I was nice to everyone. I didn't say anything rude to anybody." She put her hand over her mouth. "I told Wes and he was proud of me. Like right now I won't even tell you that today your blonde hair down looks better than your too-tight ponytail." Wow, I think to myself what a change. Then she says, "Is it okay to say too- tight ponytail or is it rude?"

Oh boy, I think to myself. "Yes, it's rude but at least you asked." I start laughing, I can't help it. "What's so funny?" Mitzy asks.

"You have no filter and somehow it strikes me funny. You have a lot of charm, you're beautiful and smart and have a fabulous sense of style. I want to know about you. Tell me your story. How did you grow up, and where? Everything you'd like to say."

Mitzy begins, "I grew up outside of Chicago in an affluent suburb. Dad and my mother were divorced. She passed away a few years ago. That's it, no siblings. I went to Northwestern and got a job at a TV station because my dad knew the owner. That's it. I moved out here because Dad got married again for the I don't know…. how many times." I listen and it makes me sad. Alex was right. Sadness is in her past. After we finish our breakfast and her story has been told, Gio comes around with the bill and she asks Gio if he has an older brother.

"I have a cousin coming to town." Mitzy is thrilled and says, "Oh good. I will be back here to meet him for sure."

Before we leave and she insists paying the check, I realize she's given me the information I needed. Her father runs a company that has done very well. She was born with a silver spoon in her mouth, in Chicago, attended Northwestern. Then she adds, "My parents drank constantly; it was a rocky environment to live in as a child. I see him on Christmas but this year I decided not to go home. I'm trying to start a new life here."

Leaving the restaurant, she winks at Gio and comments on Laurjean's attire. "Love the Christmas fashion." She smiles and heads out the door. As she waves goodbye, not looking at me, I think to myself, progress?

Chapter 13
A Dream Comes

The windy rain wakes me up in the middle of a down pour. I must have fallen back to sleep because the next thing I know my angel is holding Dukie again, pointing out a scene in my dream. Awake now, I look at the clock. It's 5 am, the usual time we get up. I feel anxious. As I recount the dream in my mind, Alex wakes up, sensing not asleep. "Good morning," I say getting out of bed.

"What is it? You've had another angel dream, haven't you?"

"Yes, the angel had Dukie in her arms and showed me a scene with at least four or five dogs in a yard. Buddy could be there. We look at the doorway. Our animals are still asleep but Winter is standing there, staring at us.

"She knows, Alex. We must go get them. The dogs are south of here, the south edge of Riverton and Dolbytown. I saw a sign."

"It's raining hard. Do you think we can wait?"

"No, it's imperative we go now. Winter, we're going soon." The other animals wake up as I get dressed quickly and Alex gets up. I tell him, "We're going to need help but everyone who offered to help like Jamie, Andy and Gio, are probably asleep or getting ready for work."

"Yes, but I think we should call them. We need Andy's van and more help if there are that many dogs."

"I don't want to call Ken unless it's a real mess."

"Gayle, call Gio now. He told me he's off today because Gus is coming to town and he'd be glad to give us a hand. You've helped him a lot."

"Okay, I will."

"I'm calling Andy to bring his van and meet us here." Alex gets dressed and I call Gio. He answers quickly in a groggy soft voice. "Gayle?"

"Yes, hi, I'm sorry to wake you. I had an angel dream again and we need to go with Winter to find dogs in a bad situation, at the south edge of Riverton. Please know you don't have to come but we need to ask Jamie too. Alex is calling Andy. We need a van."

"Gayle, yes. I'll call Jamie. We'll be over in a few." He hangs up.

"He'll get Jamie to help."

"Good, I'll get the coffee made. Maybe we should call Ken, he's asked us to."

"I hesitate calling Ken. He's done so much and has children to tend in the mornings. We need to alert Doc Jordana at some point, but it's too early to call her."

"What did you see in your dream?"

"I saw a dilapidated house on the edge of Dolbytown and dogs in the yard in the rain. One looked like a German Shepherd mix. I saw other dogs but not clearly."

Alex calls Andy.

"The guys will meet us in Andy's van in ten minutes. MJ will get the pens ready with food, water, and towels. Andy says it doesn't matter if it's raining, they're all on board."

"There may be four or more animals, I don't know. It's my psychic feeling, but Winter will be there to calm any dog we find." I'm rushing. We feed the dogs and Winter eats some food but not all of it. She knows she's got a mission to go on. I put on my coat and grab extra blankets. Alex takes Winter as we say goodbye to our animals. "We'll be back soon."

We get in my car. Alex backs out of the driveway. Winter sits in my lap. As we wait in the car, coming around the bend are the team, Andy, Jamie, and Gio.

I see the place in my mind, just as my mother did before me with the missing child. I concentrate. "South, go south. Turn two times once on Wilde Road and again on Mile Drive."

The rain is a drizzle now and the guys are close behind. Alex and I don't talk; I have to concentrate. When we get closer, I'll know. Winter will sense it and show me like she did the last two times. We drive for fifteen minutes down country roads, then we see the sign for Wilde Road. The sky is clearer as sunrise is on its way through the light rain. Alex turns and Winter starts squirming in my lap. "Almost there." I text Gio the same words. Then ahead we see Mile Drive. Alex turns and Andy turns behind us. I roll down the window and even in the drizzly rain Winter sticks her head out. We drive a mile or so and she begins barking. One bark, two barks then three. She stops and I know this is the place. It's a street with scattered houses in a rural setting. There is junk in all the yards and old wooden fences. We stop one building away from the house that I'm sure is the house where the dogs are located. It's a grey structure with small windows and a garage door that's broken off the hinges. "I'll call Andy."

Alex tells him, "Andy, stay back. Don't get out until I wave to you."

I say, "The dogs are in the back".

Alex relates this to Andy and says, "Gayle and I are going up to the door."

We get out of the car. I have Winter on her leash, and we walk on the driveway up the path then up two steps to the door. No doorbell but we knock. I hear a chorus of dogs barking in the backyard. The door opens a crack. A rough, big middle-aged man with a dark beard and wearing a dirty t-shirt and jeans says, "What do you want?" Alex does the talking. "We're here to get the dogs in the back, sir. There's been complaints."

The man laughs, "Oh, you ain't the police. Go away."

Alex waves and the three guys get out of their van now and walk up to the edge of the property. I feel nervous but somehow confident.

"Get lost." He's been drinking I can tell and doesn't seem to see the guys walking slowly toward the side of his house, but he's angry and shuts the door.

Alex and I continue to stay put. Surprisingly, the man opens the door again. "You got money for me, then I'll give 'em to you."

"We just want to get the dogs. That's all. No trouble."

"Get lost." He slams the door and it wobbles and remains slightly open.

The man looked like he wanted to hit Alex, so wordlessly I ask Ken for help. I think of him in my mind. "Ken, please come, please if you hear me. We're in trouble here with dogs who are in a hoarding situation in the back yard. Mile Drive, Riverton, on the edge of Dolbytown." I hope Ken gets my mindful prayer message. It's a miracle that the angels living as humans in Mystic Bay can suddenly appear. It's then I realize Alex is texting Ken at the same time. We stand there, and Alex has put his hand up for the guys to wait. Will the rough man get a firearm? I hope not. I pray to the angels to please help us.

It's only seems a moment before Ken comes walking down the street and up to us at the front door. He's looking bigger than ever and glowing, even though he's wearing his grey sweats. No wings in sight. How does he appear so fast? Angels in glowing flight, my mind says.

Alex knocks again and the man opens the door again. I can tell the man is intimidated now looking at Ken, his stature, his presence.

"Who are you?" the man says to Ken in astonishment. This huge angel stands before him getting larger at each moment. He must see the glow or fear the power of the angel.

"Heaven sent me," says Ken. The man looks confused and scared. Ken seems bigger as the seconds go by. Ken is such a big man but appears to be growing even larger. A staring match ensues and the gruff man begins to tremble. Then I see those same dusty sparkles that Ken sent in my car floating from his hands, surrounding the man like they surrounded Dalia. The man's shoulders relax.

Ken says in a soft voice, "We're taking the dogs now. They'll be well cared for. You did your part to help them, didn't you, Burt?"

The man starts to say something, stops and blurts out, "How did you know my name?"

We don't wait for Ken to reply. Alex takes my hand and we walk away toward the three guys who begin their way around the side of the house. Much to my surprise, when I look back at him, Ken has gone into the house. We head to the back yard. Hopefully, the gate is unlocked.

It is. Alex opens the gate and Winter enters the dump yard first and we follow. Six dogs are standing still, seemingly frightened looking at the guys and me but when they look at Winter, her calming nature must stream from her being. They all walk slowly toward her. The wind and rain have stopped, thankfully. The biggest dog, a female yellow Labrador, walks towards Winter first and lo and behold, behind her is a small cat. All the dogs and the cat are wet, dirty, and seem thin. Where did this guy Burt take them from?

Their habitat consists of a porch with blankets to sit on and an old dirty couch. The backyard has not been cleaned up and there are pans of drinking water scattered around. My eyes search each animal over as we stand there and they all gather to be close to Winter. I see two dogs that could be Buddy. One looks exactly like she's mostly German Shepherd and the other one looks similar to Dukie, light tan and black, but very timid. He is standing in the back as Winter walks around each of them, her calming influence spreading like Ken's dusty sparkles. Three little dogs, two dirty white but obviously mixes and a little black one stand close to Winter. She licks their faces. The yellow Lab stands near and seems like a sweet dog. She wags her tail and the grey cat doesn't seem scared but is glued to her dog companion's side, touching her. She's like a mama and comes with a cat! How sweet. I start to cry silently. We are all overwhelmed, but we all bend down and speak in soft voices. I say, "We are here to take you to forever homes. You are safe now."

Winter turns and starts to walk toward the gate and they all immediately follow except the dog I know is the dog I'm supposed to rescue. I bend down and outstretch my arms. "Come here, Buddy." He comes forward and places his head on my arm. I start crying. "You're Buddy, aren't you?" Does he know that name? I don't know but I've got him, the dog in my dream, and all the other dogs and a cat. So far, the gruff man hasn't come out and I know Alex is thinking what I'm thinking. I hope it's going well for Ken in the house with Burt.

Winter walks out the gate and the dogs follow her, and Buddy follows me. Gio, Andy and Jamie are just as amazed as we are watching Winter lead the way. She heads towards Andy's van.

Winter stops by the van. Andy opens the door to the back, which is covered with blankets for the animals to sit on. Jamie gets in and beckons the Lab who doesn't seem to hesitate and jumps in. She looks back and Andy has picked up the little grey cat and places her next to the dog. The bigger shepherd jumps in next. Gio picks up the little black dog and hugs her near and gets into the front. I pick up the two little white dogs and Alex tries to coax the one I believe is Buddy into the van but he stands stiff. He says, "Come on, it's okay, Buddy." Alex knows intuitively this is the dog I was meant to find. He looks like a mix with some shepherd. Buddy lets Alex put him in the van with the other animals next to Jamie.

The dogs have gone willingly. No growling or resistance. The man has stolen dogs with good dispositions. Holding the sweet, white, fluffy yet dirty little dogs, I walk to Andy's window. Andy says, "Did you see that? How is it possible? Winter is awesome and where did Ken come from?"

"I asked him to come."

"But I don't see a car." Andy is perplexed but I say, "It's near." I know Ken flew here instantly but I can't tell Andy, of course.

"Let's go now," says Andy.

"Okay, we'll meet you at your house."

"MJ will call Doc Jordana and she will come over soon." Gio has a look of wonder. He looks down at the little black dog and I know it's love at first sight. Alex has walked to my car and I go too, and we place the little dogs in the back seat with Winter beside them. I get in the back with them and we wait for Ken. The sweet dogs instantly fall asleep, safe and warm on my lap and snuggled in the blanket. They must be exhausted. Alex starts the car. "Ken will be coming."

A few moments later Ken comes out of the front door with a big Bulldog in his arms. The man, Burt, is letting Ken take his dog? This is unbelievable. Ken talks to him and the man leans over and kisses the dog on the head. The man waves as Ken and the dog get in the front. Ken nods to him. We aren't calling the police, I sense, and Ken finally speaks as we drive out away from the house. "This is Bubba, he's Burt's dog, and is in need of meds. Looks like he could have arthritis and is in need of some anti-inflammatories. I convinced Burt, I'd help him get his dog to a vet and help him with his troubles, too. Drop me off at Beach Tails Animal Hospital, okay?"

"Okay," says Alex. "Where did he get all the dogs and the little cat?"

"He took the Shepherd that you guys know is Buddy from the streets of San Francisco. He found the Lab tied to a tree in someone's yard. The cat was next to the Lab so he took the cat too. They both came willingly. He found the large Shepherd by the side of the road a week ago. The two white dogs were given to him by somebody at a bar. They were in the man's truck and he didn't want them anymore. He was going to get rid of them, he told Burt. Burt couldn't care for them like he wanted to, though, since he only works once in a while at odd jobs and his wife left him because of the animals. He told me he tries his best but he's running out of money for food. He found the little black dog all alone near a dumpster in Dolbytown."

"I told him we'd find homes for the dogs and cat and that I'll bring his Bubba back today with dog food and medicine. I convinced him not to get anymore dogs or cats but I'll be counselling him at his house once a week. I'll bring him coffee and bagels today and some more food. I'll come over on Christmas too, I told him. We need to get some volunteers to help him clean up his place."

Alex says, "You know I'll help."

"Thank you, Alex. I hope to help him get a job. He said all those dogs needed help and he knows he's been depressed, since his wife left months ago."

I say, "That's when Buddy was taken."

Alex says to Ken, "I heard you tell him to believe angels were near and he said he believed you might be an angel!"

"Yes, he did, Alex. Of course, I told him I was sent by an angel and he believed me. But I'm intrigued. You heard me, even though you were in the back yard. You have an angel's ear. What a blessing. Do you use it often?"

I'm shocked as Alex never told me about this.

"I didn't know it had come back. I could hear things from the next room or far away when I was a child, but it went away, I thought as I got older. Perhaps I haven't needed to use it until now."

Ken says, "An angel's ear is a gift from above. What else are you hearing? Alex is silent for a moment or two but then says, "I'm hearing the calm breathing in the backseat of the animal's and their heartbeats. I can hear Gayle's heart and yours too, Ken. Your heartbeat is so slow, like no human being, I am guessing!"

"Ah," laughs Ken. "Bubba here can hear my heartbeat, too. The dogs know I'm an angel and you know dogs are a type of angel too, all animals are. Animals are teachers to us all."

My heart is full thinking of what Ken just said. It's so profound I can't speak, as we drive along in silence. Andy follows close behind. Winter has calmed the dogs. I see sparkling dust Ken is sending us all. I am overwhelmed at this miracle my dream produced and so very much relieved. I look at the little dogs' closed eyes and know we'll keep them if no one wants them.

The little white dogs snuggle in the warmth next to my coat and as near to Winter as possible. Ken has spread his sparkling calm around all of us and he's probably sending it over in angel dust to Andy's van. I feel my eyes close as we head toward Andy's rescue where MJ will be waiting with clean places ready for the dogs and cat. Jordana will heal not only with her medicines but with her healing touch. I don't need to even talk with Alex; we will take Buddy. I realize I loved Buddy before I met him, from the moment I knew Vince didn't want him. It comes to me that Maggie and Noah might love the little white ones snuggled here. Otherwise, we will take them in. The Lab and cat? We'll take them if no one else does. Ken must be reading my thoughts.

"Gayle, the cat is attached to the Lab. They go together and we will find them a special home."

Alex says, "The others will find homes. Jamie will take one, Gio too. It's written in the clouds and stars. Am I right, Ken?"

"Oh, so right," Ken says.

The window wipers swish, the wind is calm, and we've done it. With the help of an angel, we've rescued dogs and a cat and Alex and I have found another dog to love. More love? We have plenty of that.

Chapter 14
Leading Them Home

It's been the busiest of days. At Andy's rescue, the scene was relatively tranquil, considering MJ had everything prepared. Bobbi and Lulu are living in Andy and MJ's house now and Doc Jordana was there tending to every one of the animals. The yellow Lab and the kitty were put together. Buddy, the little white dogs, and the little black dog were put together. The other Shepherd mix was the last to be examined and placed in with the Lab and kitty. They were fed first then washed up. They didn't seem to mind it. Jordana washed the cat with warm towels and the other dogs willingly went into the nice warm tubs. They all were filthy. We had dropped Ken off at the vet hospital so Doc Josh could tend to Bubba. Alex and I helped towel dry each dog and patted them to sleep in soft beds. Kitty, as I called her, snuggled with her Lab and they all were content. The one we call Buddy seemed still skittish but lay next to the little dogs and Winter lay next to them all day. She did rounds of love to each.

"This day is beyond extraordinary," said Andy to me. Alex left before I did to let the dogs out and Jamie went to work. Gio left to meet Gus for the first time at their new apartment above Ken's store.

Ken texted me; he was going back to Burt's and bringing Donnie with him. He told me Gio and Gus were at the apartment and loved it. Donnie and Ken will help Burt today by talking to him about adjusting to the animals' leaving and the grief he's enduring from his wife's departure. They will help plan for a better life for him and Bubba. Burt will never know that two loving angels are guiding him in real time.

I stayed most of the day and Alex picked me up at five. We had to leave Buddy, knowing he'll be ours soon but needs immunizations and rest with the dogs he knows. It's overwhelming to them all, I'm sure, yet I'm convinced they feel rescued. They've all been through trauma. Buddy actually looked at me with love in his eyes as I petted him and said goodbye. Like Gio, it was love at first sight for me. I promised the little white dogs that I've a home in mind they will love. I took photos of them and texted Maggie. She texted back that she and Noah would be thrilled to adopt them. That's what love does. It does miraculous things.

Chapter 15

Home Again

When we come home with Winter, we are all tired but so glad to be home. The dogs and cat run to us. Alex sits on the couch and Magic and Maurice pounce on him, and Ralph is at his side waiting for glorious pets.

But I am surprised when I sit by Winter's bed by the fireplace and she licks my hand. Her head is bowed low and she actually places her head on my lap. We stay there a while as Alex and I talk of the amazing rescue.

"It's unbelievable how you dreamed of the scene and found where the animals were. Clearly, your abilities are getting stronger. It's astounding that Winter knew which house the dogs were in again, the same way she found Lulu and Bobbi. She comforted all the dogs and it is beyond incredible each time to witness. You two are connected in a phenomenal way."

"I think she is bonding with us both and knew somehow Buddy was going to be ours too. The dog is Buddy but there is no absolute proof unless I take him to see Vince, but I think that's not a good idea. I'll take a photo. We didn't discuss it, but we're keeping, Buddy, right?"

"Of course, Gayle, and if the other dogs or the cat need a home, we'll take them too." I tell him, "Maggie and Noah are interested in the little white dogs and I'm thrilled. But the Labrador and her kitty, could we take them too?"

"If no one comes forward we will. What's four dogs and two cats? There's always room for one more. Hey, it's coming to me maybe your mom and dad will take the Lab and her kitty."

"Alex, that's the best idea. I'm calling them now over at Aunt Nancy and Uncle Dick's. They're bringing over a casserole Aunt Nancy made. Yay! I don't have to cook. You can tell them the story of today."

My parents and aunt and uncle arrive with food and drink. We sit at the table and talk about the miracle of today and Mom and Dad are excited to go to Andy's tomorrow morning to see the yellow Lab and cat. "The cat's got to be named Kitty, for sure," says Mom. Dad pipes in, "I always wanted a Lab. I'll name him Brutus."

I laugh at that. "Dad, the Lab is a girl. She is almost the color of, well, almost gold."

"Well then, we'll call her Cleo, for her goldish color. Right, Marie, Cleopatra? The Egyptian queen is your favorite?" My mom laughs. "Sure, Ted, great idea."

I sigh the relief sigh as the evening goes on. When dinner is over, our family heads home as everyone, human, and animal are yawning in our household. There is a side gate between the houses and walking into the yard with animals in tow, we look at the stars above.

Alex says, "Clouds covering the moon look like see through scarves flowing in the night."

"Yes, how beautiful it is. Christmas Eve tomorrow. We breathe in the cold sea air as the animal crew roams around the yard. We see Aunt Nancy and Uncle Dick's lights turn on in their bedroom and the guest room lights turn on in the upstairs bedroom where Mom and Dad will retire. We go into the house for much needed sleep for us and for Winter. She goes to her place by the fireplace and as usual I go to say goodnight to her. "I love you always, sweet Winter." Her eyes are heavy but her tail wags in response. As the other animals file into our room, I wonder if the dog, Buddy, will want to sleep with us or with Winter his first night. It's not really important, of course, because I know that love is all that matters and Buddy, the dog I was meant to find will finally have a home.

Chapter 16

Surprises On Christmas Eve

We awake to a foggy Christmas Eve day and much to do. Last night my mother told me, "Soon, Gayle, I see Winter coming to your bedroom. It's a matter of time." My mother is so intuitive and she and my dad will go with us to Andy's this morning and look to adopt Cleo and Kitty. My dad said, "Maybe we can take more of them home with us. One more dog, more to love."

We go with them to say hi to Buddy and see the rest of the dogs and Kitty too. Buddy is happy to see us. We want to take him home today but think it will be too much for him because of the party today. My mom thinks so. Andy agrees and we decide to let him rest today. Christmas morning will be a great time to come home. Maggie and Noah, Jamie, Laurjean and Donnie, and Gio and Gus will pick up their dogs tomorrow too. But now they all are exhausted and need to be together.

I bend down to talk to Buddy. "See you tomorrow, Buddy. We're taking you home." He wags his tail as if he knows he's safe. Maybe he knows what home means. We leave and Mom and Dad offer to pick up the sandwiches we're going to serve today from Mystic Bay Cheese and Wine Store. It's a busy day but I have to meet Mitzy. She wanted to get together for coffee at The Next Door Café. Wes called me yesterday thanking me. "She's improving, Gayle." That makes me feel good. As we drive home, I ask Alex, "Should I invite Mitzy to come to our open house? She's allergic to dogs."

"Yes, invite her over for sure. She can always say no but you've done a great job."

"I didn't really do anything, just hints. She doesn't have a filter."

Alex laughs, "I have an idea she'll come. I'll meet you out front of the restaurant at ten and then we'll meet your parents over at the store. Their van will fit all we ordered. Maybe we'll pick up more wine too."

As we go in the house, I say, "I ordered corned beef, roast beef, chicken and tuna salad and homemade peanut butter and jelly for the kids. Winter, we're having our first annual Trim-the-Tree-party. You guys will have fun, except you Maurice. You'd better hide about three o'clock."

Alex laughs at that. "Put red bows on the dogs, and even Maurice. They'll circle around the dining room table, hoping the kids drop chips and cookies on the floor."

As I clean up the kitchen and get ready for company, I think of Mitzy. Will it be the last time we meet? Is she really improving? I don't know.

Alex and I discuss picking up Buddy Christmas morning but realize he'll have to pick Buddy up alone. I'll be leaving for the shelter by eight.

I finish putting out the paper plates and getting the Christmas table set. The tree is filled with white lights and gold trimming waiting for the ornaments to grace its beauty. The box of ornaments is out for people to choose from. I put the German Shepherd ornament Ken gave me on the tree, high enough for me to see as I pass by. We can't wait for Buddy to come home tomorrow. He's such a sweet guy, he will fit right into our family. I explain to Alex, "I've decided to tell Vince about Buddy. I'll show him the photo I took of him. And when I get a chance, I'll ask Jerome about Winter's past too. I can't be afraid of information about Winter's past or if Vince has changed his mind about Buddy."

"Good idea, Gayle." But after I kiss my husband, pet the animals and look at Winter's melancholy eyes, I wonder out loud, "What if Jerome has found Winter's companion? I can't think about that."

Alex says, "Let's hope everything will work out just fine." As I walk out the door my angels put the thought in my mind, "*Love always wins.*"

My walk is a brisk one to The Next Door Café this Christmas Eve. The walk fills my heart with the spirit of the season. It's chilly this morning but people are out and about and the place is packed. The smell of breakfast cooking fills the air. I see neighbors and stop to talk but Laurjean has my back table all ready for us and beckons me back over. She's wearing her traditional Mrs. Santa dress, red with a white faux fur trim, red bow in her hair, green tights, and red flats. She looks so great. Her green hair has more streaks in it. She pours me a cup of coffee and sashays her way around. I see Mitzy walk in looking lovely as usual. Designer white sweater, trimmed in silver and white jeans, with a white faux fur jacket. Funny to me, I've worn my white sweater too, but mine has a big Christmas tree on the front. My white jeans aren't designer like hers. I have silver bells on my ears. Yes, I love Christmas. Everyone in the restaurant has something Christmassy on.

Mitzy was a runway model in Chicago and it shows. But there's something different about her today. The glum expression has gone. There's a lightness to her step this morning in her black high heel boots. She laughs when she greets Laurjean, "You're hysterical!"

"I try, kiddo," says Laurjean. The merriment in the restaurant is infectious and loud too. Mitzy is on time today and I'm wondering what she wants to talk about. I guess I'm breaking through her stone unfilterness, if there is such a word. If not, I made it up. Maybe she's softened a tad and hopefully, it's enough for her to keep her job. Heads turn as she walks by tables coming up to ours.

"Mitzy," I get up laughing. "Will you look at the two of us, it's as if we called each other to wear white or went shopping together, although your outfit is absolutely gorgeous as always."

"I see," she says smiling an enthusiastic smile. "I do look good. But, well, you look great too."

"Thank you. I remember you usually critique my clothing"

"Yes, but no more. It must be that your psychic vibe is catching like a fever. I'm learning to be, well, better." She sits down. I'm hoping she's serious.

Laurjean, in her Mrs. Santa dress, pours her coffee. Mitzy looks her up and down again and tells her, "Laurjean, you go for hilarious and you got it, lady!"

As Laurjean bustles away, she says to Mitzy, "Merry Christmas to you too, you beautiful creature!" Then Gio arrives wearing a Christmas Next Door Café Santa t-shirt.

"Good morning. What will your order be, ladies?"

Mitzy says with a smile, "Eggs Benedict, Gio. Love the Christmas tee."

"Thanks, Laurjean always has t-shirt themes. And you Miss Gayle?"

"The usual, Gio. I was going to just have coffee but I'm starved. Thank you."

"Gus and I moved in yesterday afternoon, after we all rescued the dogs and cat. Gus is such a great guy. Hey, we were going to tell you tonight but go down Main Street after you finish here to see him at our new business. It's right next to Bondo Bikes. It's a surprise! We can't wait for you to see it!!"

"Really, okay we will. This is great news!"

"Oh, and Gayle. Another surprise. We're bringing Kia, the little black dog, home tomorrow. She's our Christmas gift to each other. Gus fell in love with her right away when I took him over to see her last night."

"How wonderful. We're picking up Buddy tomorrow, too. Well, Alex is. I have to work. All the animals found homes. Let's talk tonight, you're busy now."

"You got that right." He walks away with our order. I'm thankful that Gio seems so very happy and that he's adopted Kia too.

I'm lost in thought drinking my coffee when Mitzy says, "You rescue dogs too? What, always good works on your calendar?" I don't have time to respond because she goes on, "I'm working tomorrow too with Chase because it's Christmas and I have nothing else to do. I'll see you on air."

"Do you have any family or friends here?"

"No friends or family." Mitzy's look is a sad one now. What a shame she has nowhere to go or anyone to be with. I should ask her to come over tonight, but she's allergic to dogs. Alex said to ask her anyway, so I say, "Mitzy, would you like to come over today to our open house from three on? We're just inviting family and some friends for food and drinks."

Before Mitzy can answer Ken is miraculously at our table. "Hello Gayle."

"Ken, I didn't see you."

"I'm just getting coffee to go before I head toward my store. Busy day today." He looks at Mitzy and smiles.

"Ken, this is Mitzy Blane, my co-worker." Mitzy stands and seems thrilled to see him.

"Coach Ken of the San Francisco Shakers? I met you when I was ten. My dad, Ed Blane, is a part owner of the Shakers."

"Mitzy, I do remember meeting you when you were a little girl. Your dad is such a nice man. How is Ed doing? He hasn't been here in a long time."

"Well, I don't see my father much. He's remarried again for the sixth time." She looks at him with a sad expression, a disappointed one.

"Mitzy, I own a store down the street called Heaven Can't Wait. Walk over when you've finished your breakfast. I'm sure Gayle will show you where it is, okay? I'd like to give you something."

"Oh well, thank you," Mitzy says with great enthusiasm. Ken walks away but I see the little floating dusty angel light that he seems to send to those in need of comfort. The sparkly dusts float around Mitzy. Can anyone else see them? Everyone around us is eating and talking and oblivious. The floating starry snowflakes drift like whisps toward me. I take a deep breath and close my eyes. I feel calmer. I open my eyes and see Mitzy's eyes are closed too. Then she opens them and blinks, looking at me.

"He's such a good man."

"He is totally wonderful. His counselling has helped change many lives. He's counseled at Bay Star Shelter for years." Of course, I can't tell her Ken is a real angel and how lucky we are to have him in our lives. Then I wonder, how did he know I was here with Mitzy? Did Alex tell him I was here? Of course, he did.

I'm about to ask her again about coming over even with her dog allergy, I want her to feel welcome but just then a very pregnant Maggie, with Noah and Marshall, come to our table. I introduce them to Mitzy. Maggie says, "You are prettier in real life, Mitzy. You do such a great job. We watch you every weekend, without fail."

"Tomorrow, I'll be doing the traffic when you check in. I'm working Christmas this year, new kid on the block, you know."

"Maggie's been my best friend since we were kids and Noah is a writer. He's done documentaries and written books about the angel sightings by children in this town and his newest one is just out, about people who have seen angels."

"Is this town for real? It's like Mayberry, RFD, the nicest town ever? I watched that show when I was a kid plugged into the TV. Angels appearing to kids? You've got to tell me all about this, Gayle."

"I'll bring some copies of my new books tonight, Gayle for everyone," Noah tells us. Then he adds, "It's nice meeting you." They leave for their table. Our breakfast comes and I must wait until after we eat to ask Mitzy again if she'll come over today for our party.

We both seem ravenous piling in to our breakfast and while we're eating, she tells me again how Wes is pleased with her and says he sees a difference. "But it's a lie going around that Wes owed my dad a favor and that's why he hired me. I wasn't fired just politely asked to leave. Wes knew my dad because of the Shakers. My dad showed him my resume and a some of my work and Wes told Dad he needed a traffic person for weekends. In Chicago, I was just a reporter for the morning news out shlepping in the early Chicago morning. It was freezing in the winter and brutal in the summer. I wasn't fired. Well... they didn't like me there really, and I needed a break from my father and his new young wife, younger than me. The station didn't even give me a party to send me off although I worked there for two years. My fans loved me, loved my clothes. They email me here too. But Dad didn't even care that I moved. He had the packers load my stuff and move me fast, found an expensive condo in Hillsboro and swish, here I am."

I find I don't know how to respond but Mitzy begins again eating with gusto. Gio comes by asking how our food is. "Scrumptious," says Mitzy with a mouthful.

More friends I know stop by our table to say hello and most of them recognize Mitzy as well from our weekend news. Everyone compliments her, telling her they love watching us and she beams with pride. I still want to talk to her about our open house but we are finished and Gio leaves the bill and clears the table. Mitzy swipes it before I can. "I'm buying again today. Thank you for your help. I don't think I need mentoring anymore, though. I have listened to everything you've said and I'm trying to apply it in every situation at work, restaurants, everywhere."

"I'm grateful Mitzy, I can tell the difference. Remember, you have an enormous amount of talent."

"Thanks."

"'Really, all I did was give you a few pointers."

"No, it's more than that. I watched how you interact with everyone here and at work, the tone, and the kind ways, even to me when I was being well... rude. You made me think about a lot of things like how the other person feels about our grandmother's perfume. You seemed hurt."

I tell her, "I love my grandmother still and yes, I guess I was more baffled than hurt wondering why you say the things you do."

"I don't know, really." She looks away.

Then I say something that surprises me. "Let's get together some Mondays like this when we're both free."

"Really? I could use the company."

"Great. Thank you for breakfast."

She leaves cash on the table with a large tip for Gio, winking at him as she tells him to keep the rest and we get up to leave. "My husband Alex is outside so I'd like you to meet him and I'm hoping you'll come to our house later today."

"We'll see."

I'm glad I asked but Winter is outside. Alex will keep her back from Mitzy. We make our way out of the restaurant. There are a lot of patrons, old and new friends wishing Merry Christmas to each other. I hug Laurjean telling her how I appreciate the homey wonderful place, and that I'm sorry they can't come today to our open house. But she tells me, "Thank you, Gayle for finding the adorable Elfie and babies. My son will take the other two puppies. We pick them up in a few weeks. It is indeed a wonderful Christmas. I have gifts at my house for the shelter. Donnie will pop by later to deliver them to your house. Maybe he can stay for a glass of beer."

I open the door for us and it's chilly but there he is, my husband holding furry, white Magic with one arm and he's got Winter close to him on the leash. I immediately take Magic in my arms. "Alex, this is Mitzy."

"Mitzy, I've heard so much about you." Alex offers his sincere smile that I love and she says laughing, "I bet you have. Why Gayle, now I know why you dumped that what's-his-name, Detective Beau."

Embarrassed, but laughing, Alex looks at me smiling, "Glad, she did."

Alex tells Mitzy, "This is Winter, and Magic, The Weather Dog. Gayle says you're allergic." Mitzy is looking intently at Winter now. "Why her eyes are mesmerizing, but I can't pet her. I'm not allergic, really, just scared of dogs. My parents never let me have one. Bring Magic to work, Gayle, I just won't touch her. Her fur looks better than on the billboard."

My intuition didn't pick this up. I won't mention that she lied to our boss and caused me to change my weekend location forecasts with Magic. "I would appreciate you telling Wes so he confirms it's okay. Magic is a sweet girl and Winter is a comfort dog to other dogs, cats and humans. They are both rescues and wouldn't hurt anyone."

"Well, of course I'll tell Wes. I get to keep my job now because of you. I'd like to come to your party. Text me your address, please. Now, which way to Ken's store?" I tell her where, pointing down Main Street and she says goodbye and smiles at us. Off she goes clip clopping with those high boots of hers down the street. "She's changed, Alex, I didn't see it happening."

"I did. It came to me she wasn't really allergic just needed you to be her guide to figure this all out. She was alienating those around her. That's what I saw. But this is super."

"Did you ask Ken to come by the restaurant?"

"Yep. I told him what I thought and somehow, I knew he'd float those little whatever he does, angel dust, around her and invite her to his store. I thought maybe she'd even come clean about her being allergic."

"Your intuition just gave me back my Magic, The Weather Dog! Next weekend we'll be ready. Now, we've got to go down the street. Mom and Dad are picking up the sandwiches but Gio says Gus is in their new store by Bondo Bikes. We don't have to wait until later to see him. I wonder what his business is?"

"Really? Let's go find out."

We walk down the street and certainly Christmas is in the air with such brisk weather and the bustle of the day. It makes people walk faster. Tomorrow night is the annual parade but we will miss it. Buddy will be ours and we'll spend a quiet Christmas with our family at our house, low key for him so he can get used to us. We see Mom and Dad driving away down Main Street. "Mom and Dad picked up the sandwiches, Alex."

"Look," he says. We stop walking in disbelief. There it is a sign on the building next to Bondo Bikes, Coming Soon: Main Street Coffee. Alex tries the door and it's open. Behind a counter and in the almost empty store, there he is. Gus, aka Guiseppi, greets us. He looks totally changed with his short hair dyed platinum blonde, his dark beard standing out in contrast, but that handsome face I recognize, is beaming. He has a big smile for us. "Gayle, my angel! Hey Alex."

Gus comes over and gives me a hug and shakes Alex's hand. He bends down to the dogs. "Who are your furry friends?"

"This is Winter and this is Magic, The Weather Dog."

"Oh, I remember Magic on TV and on the billboards. Hey, thank you for finding our dog, our Kia, too. We pick her up tomorrow and she's going to go everywhere with us. This is our store, and we'll have a little bed for her here."

Alex says, "It's great you're opening a coffee shop. Finally, a coffee shop in Mystic Bay. There really is no place except restaurants to get coffee here. "

"Yay, I'm a true coffee lover and so is Gio. We decided to have a coffee shop and sell our Grandma Maria's Italian cookies and biscotti from her old recipe. Tyler Parker is our silent partner and investor. He told me if I hadn't come forward, the case would have not gone as well and his father might have actually, well... died. He has helped me so much like the older brother I never had. I am indebted to him. Plus, finding Gio has changed my life and my Aunt Talia's. It's all come together because I met you, Gayle."

He looks at me with such emotion and I feel overwhelmed too. I can hardly speak but must: "Gus, this is great. We're so happy for you both."

"Thanks. We have a lot of work to do. We hope to open Valentines' Day and we're going to name a coffee after you both. Gayle. What's your favorite coffee drink?"

"Really? Well, my favorite is nonfat latte."

"That's what it'll be."

"And Alex, your favorite?"

"Espresso!"

"Alex's Espresso. You got it!"

Gus takes us around the store and back kitchen area. Gio will do the baking and keep his two jobs until such time as he can work full-time at the store, to be open daily from six until six.

Alex congratulates him, saying, "This is truly wonderful and you guys are our neighbors now. You're coming for the open house today?"

"Wouldn't miss it, thank you. We love our apartment and with picking up little Kia tomorrow.... well ...it's like I'm living my dream."

"Are you safe now, Gus? I'm worried."

"As safe as can be. I've a new identity, Gayle. I promise."

We leave, hopeful for the two worthy cousins to be happy here, having a fresh start.

The sandwiches are in the fridge when we get home and we start to get ready for our party with Mom, Dad, Aunt Nancy and Uncle Dick's help. Winter and Magic are tired. Ralph goes for a walk with Alex and we all sit for a moment when he gets back, wishing for a nap but we all have to get dressed.

At exactly three my parents and aunt and uncle come back over and simultaneously the doorbell rings. Magic and Ralph bark but wise Winter gets up with joy. The angels send me a message in my mind for a moment. "*Winter hopes someone is coming.*" Winter looks happy like the other dogs. I know she still misses her someone special. I'll talk to Jerome about her tomorrow.

Chapter 17

Trimming The Tree Party

Everyone piles in at once, as they all have family parties to go to. MJ, Andy and Jamie and his daughter come in at the same time. They're all having dinner together at Andy's parents' house. Jamie is adopting the other Shepherd, we rescued, naming her Riley. Everyone is talking about the rescue and adoption and Andy is thrilled that Mom and Dad will take Cleo and Kitty home.

Gus and Gio come in when Mitzy arrives and the party is getting started. Mitzy doesn't seem afraid of the dogs anymore, which astounds me.

The food helps with the merriment and it's a complete party when Maggie, Noah, and Marshall come in. Maurice hides under the red chair, hoping no one will see him.

Jamie's little girl, Emma Rose, sits down with Winter and pets her head. So sweet to see.

Ken and Jordana pop in to wish us a Merry Christmas and have brought their little girl, May, and son, Val. They are going to host their own dinner but wanted to stop by. Ken gives us a little ornament for our tree. Amazingly, it's a black and white dog like Winter. They say their hellos, the kids have cookies and then the children pet all the dogs. I see Ken's introduced his family to Mitzy and she seems so happy. After they leave, Mitzy tells me. "I stayed all day in your town after going to Ken's store. Would you believe he gave me a beautiful blue-winged porcelain angel to keep!" It's then the thought comes from the angels through my mind: *"Her guardian angel has blue wings!"*

The food is eaten, only a few ornaments are left to put on the tree and Mitzy is sitting down on the couch with Maggie and Noah. Noah has given her his newly published book. He has one for all of us. Gus and Gio sit on the floor as everyone else finds a place to sit. Sitting down on the living room couch, Noah begins reading the first chapter from, *They Believe They Saw Angels*.   Noah begins...

Chapter One   Cliff's Angel

He was on a lonely road late at night. His old car broke down, and there were no cell phones years ago. Just a young man with no one to help him, no job, no money and no one to hope he would come home on this cold, wintry night. But out of nowhere, a young man came, a black man like himself. He stopped his truck and got out. "Trouble?" he asked Cliff.

Cliff told him he couldn't get his car started and didn't know what was wrong. The man went straight to work. With no tools he seemed to quickly fix whatever was wrong with the engine. The man said, "It should work now, start it."

Cliff started the car and turned to say thank you to the man but he was nowhere in sight. No truck, no man disappearing in the night. Cliff told me, "All these years later, knowing the man most likely was an angel sent to help me seems like nothing short of a miracle. Appearing so quickly to come to my aid and then disappearing as soon as the engine worked, it changed my life. I decided that if there are angels out there, helping people like me, then I will try to be like them if that's possible. I will help my fellow man in whatever way I can. I will find a full and happy life because once when I was in need...heaven sent a real angel my way."

We all love the story and everyone is given a book of their own. I don't look at Maggie, Noah, or Alex as we all know the secret of this wonderful story. Noah met Cliff at Ken's house one day when he was starting the manuscript. Cliff kept going on and on how it was a real coincidence that years later he thought his angel looked like a young Coach Ken. But then he told Noah, "It was a young man and you know Coach is older. I'm sure angels don't grow old."

The four of us know the real truth is that when angels come down from heaven to live a human life, they grow old like the rest of us mortals. When they want to return to heaven, whenever it is during their time on earth, they go back to the form they were in, whether it be younger or older. How special it is that Cliff turned his life around because one day he met an angel, and Ken was the angel that came his way. A beautiful image of the scene runs through my mind.

With a "Merry Christmas," Jamie leaves with Emma Rose who carries her little angel doll everywhere. In my heart, and Alex's too, we figured out that Jamie's Emma Rose was the little girl who saw an angel as Maggie babysat her a few years ago. Maggie never would tell me, but I know she knows we figured it out. The children's angel encounters were a miracle story from Mystic Bay.

My parents and aunt and uncle are in the kitchen cleaning up when the only people left in the room are Mitzy, Gio and Gus with Maggie, Noah and their little boy. Gio gets his nerve up to speak, "I have a story. It's how I came to know Gus, my cousin. It's the miracle of my childhood and I want to tell it to you."

As Gio tells the story of his grandmother Maria's spirit comforting him as a little boy and then again as a teen, I glance at Mitzy sitting by Maggie. She seems so engaged. Noah asked Gio if his new book could add the story and of course Gio says yes. "All my life, I waited for knowledge about my family and an angel sent my grandma. She was Gus' too. Gus and I met because of her spirit and the kindness of others along our way. To be living here in this town passes all my expectations."

Gus says, "It's the miracle of Mystic Bay isn't it. Of course, and the people who live here like Gayle and Alex and all of you." He turns and glances and Mitzy and smiles. She notices and smiles a beautiful smile in return. I think, oh really? These two need to know each other better, maybe over a cup of coffee when Gio and Gus' Main Street Coffee opens? I store that plan away in the notebook in my brain.

After the discussion, gaiety and goodbyes fill our house with friendship and love. As I look around the room in reflection, Mitzy walks into the kitchen, talking away to my mom and Aunt Nancy. Uncle Dick is in deep conversation with Noah and my dad. It's then I look at Winter sitting in her bed near Ralph by the fire. I think I see the spirit of my father; he's smiling that smile I see every day in the photograph by my bedside. The flash of his face is gone but I know he is near. Even though I never met him and will have to wait until my journey here on earth is over, I know he is near. Once in a while I have a moment of insight that brings me joy. These moments help me figure things out. Alex must have seen me lost in thought and comes over to me. "Are you okay?"

"Just saw my father's spirit for a moment and it made me happy. I'm glad to see this party went so well, and to think we get to have Buddy home with us tomorrow. I need to show Vince his photo though."

"Okay, but what if he wants him?"

"I'll decide what to say. I have to ask Jerome tomorrow if he's found out anything about Winter's companion too."

My mom comes up to us and says, "I heard you talk about Buddy. We will pick up Cleo and Kitty tomorrow too. Nancy and Dick say it's fine. Prince will be okay but we'll have to keep Kitty in the guest room because Dick's allergic to cats. You guys did a great job this Christmas. I'm so grateful we have kids like you."

"Apples don't fall far from the tree," my dad pipes in walking up to us."

Uncle Dick, Aunt Nancy, and Mitzy join us. Alex says to all in the room, "It's going to be a great Christmas Day. The angels sent Gayle on journeys and those of us on her coattails got lucky, our Christmas stockings come with rescued dogs and a kitty too."

The merriment continues as everyone stays until seven then leaves for home to celebrate the rest of their Christmas Eve together but Mitzy is the last one to leave.

Walking her to the door, I notice that Mitzy's look has softened. "I brought you something," she says. From her purse she pulls out a little white box with a red ribbon on it. "Mitzy, you shouldn't have."

"Yes, I should have. Come on open it."

I open the little box and there inside are tiny gold drop angel earrings. "Why Mitzy these are beautiful. Thank you."

"I was going to give them to you this morning, but I waited until the party. My late grandmother gave them to me many years ago. I never wear them. I guess they've been waiting for you. You live in a town where kids have seen angels. You've been trying to help me, and I think you are an angel on earth that luckily came my way. Maybe you could wear them tomorrow to the shelter Christmas party? I'd love to see them with your crazy green Christmas sweatshirt." She laughs. She walks out the door after I've thanked her again then turns around. "By the way, I'm not afraid of dogs anymore. I looked into Winter's eyes as she sat by the fire and such a loving soul changed my way of thinking. She has been hurt emotionally and you saved her life. Keep saving lives human and furry. See you on air tomorrow!" Then she is off to her sportscar. I watch her drive away. Who would have thought that tomorrow, Christmas Day, would be a day of change for the animals at Andy's Rescue and also for Mitzy Blane? I guess the angels could see it. The angels, just like Ken.

Chapter 18
Christmas Day

I'm on-air at the shelter every thirty minutes for the morning update. People are pouring in this breakfast shift this morning of eggs, bacon, pancakes and more. When they're finished with their breakfast, the kids will head over to see Santa Jerome sitting in a big chair with presents all around.

I'm standing with Director Ronna and business man, Tyler Parker. I interview Tyler Parker first. "Tyler, you've put on three shifts of families and others who get to enjoy this beautiful breakfast, complete with Santa too. Tell me how you feel right now." "Well, Gayle," he answers, "it truly is a Merry Christmas. Fifty families and singles have moved into our new apartments this week and they're celebrating the holidays with homes and hope. More homes for others are on the way. We have a great lunch with Santa too. The generosity from donors and people all around the Bay has been overwhelming. We are thankful for the furniture, and clothes and toys and items for the apartments. Ronna here has been at the helm and she is one giving human being, an angel in our midst. My heart is full."

"Ronna, what are you feeling right now?"

"Thankful, full of gratitude to Tyler Parker and the outpouring of Christmas love and spirit from the community. This is a day filled with joy!"

As we talk on, Saul pans the camera to catch everyone eating. We finish with Santa Jerome entering the room. We won't show the kids individual faces but the public will see the impact this has made for all.

"Back to you Chase and Mitzy...I'll report again in thirty minutes."

Chase says, "It's wonderful Gayle. Don't you think Mitzy?"

"It's extraordinary. There are angels all around, Gayle. Even on your ears." I hear her voice filled with happiness as my angel earrings dangle and dance.

When Santa has given out the gifts and all the shifts of people have left the building, I find a chance to talk to Jerome.

"Jerome, you were a fabulous Santa." His jolly disposition shows. "I have a question. I wonder if you think it would be alright to show Vince a photo, I took of the dog I'm sure is Buddy. He's coming home with us today and I am wondering if Vince will recognize him and yet I wonder if he will ask to take him."

"Gayle," Jerome says with kindness, "Vince isn't capable of taking care of the dog. He finds them wandering in the streets because he has a kind heart but we find them homes. He may recognize Buddy and if he does just tell him that Buddy has a forever home with a nice family."

"Okay, thank you. I was hoping you would say that."

"I'd love to come see Buddy, to meet him and see Winter. Would that be, okay?"

"Are you kidding? We'd love it. Please come soon."

"Great, I will."

"One more thing. Do you know anything about Winter's companion, the man?"

"Just what I learned when I asked around. He left one day but no one saw him. He lived on the streets briefly. We are thinking he passed away. It takes time for dogs to know they're home after they've been rescued." He gives me a hug and goes to talk to some adults still sitting at the tables drinking coffee. Alex has texted me that all went well with getting Buddy home, and I for one can't wait to get back to my new addition and little family but I have one last thing to accomplish.

Vince is working but I ask the chef if I can have a word with him. Vince walks over, wiping his hands on a towel. "Hi Vince. Merry Christmas to you." I pull my phone from my jeans and show him the photo of Buddy. "This dog has found a forever home now and I'm wondering if this is the dog you found that you called Buddy?"

Vince looks at it a while. "Yes, that's him. But I can't take him, you know."

"I know that Vince and I thank you. Because of you, many dogs have been rescued. Thank you for helping us save them."

"No problem," Vince says and walks away to continue his job. I sigh a sigh of relief. Buddy is ours.

Our Christmas present was bringing Buddy home this morning, all because of my dream. Maggie texted they named the little dogs Amber and Angie. She sent a photo of the delight on Marshall's face holding the dogs while he sat on the floor. I say goodbye and Merry Christmas to all.

I drive home with sea air coming through a crack in the window. When I turn onto Main Street. I give a heartfelt sigh of happiness to be home where I belong. I walk in the house and out to the patio. Winter, Maurice, Magic and Ralph are outside with Alex and Buddy. He seems timid but stands close to Winter. Alex is kneeling down petting him, "Buddy. Here's Mom." I walk to him and kneel beside him. "Hello Buddy. Welcome home!"

Chapter 19
The Dog Who Came For Christmas

Alex is already sleeping this Christmas night, exhausted from the big day but I just can't, thinking about my own life as a mortal married to a half-angel, kind husband. An angel in a dream holding dear Dukie sent me on mission, a miraculous mission to help lives. I look out the window and see stars glittering down from above. Maurice, Buddy, Ralph and Magic are asleep too. Maurice, as always, is snug with Magic and Ralph cozies in his own bed. Buddy wanted to sleep in our room. He looked back at Winter as if to say, "Aren't you coming?" But Winter stayed back by the glow of the fire. I wonder if Winter will ever come to our room to sleep with us. Will she disappear when Christmas is over? Is she really an angel dog? For this whole time in our home, she's been nestled by the fireplace and I've stopped asking her to join us, as I know she waits for someone to return.

I close my eyes now, hoping sleep will come. I'm not dreaming. My Angel whispers to me. I sit up, breathless hearing her clearly, knowing she is in the room with me this time and not just in my dreams or with her words running through my mind.

"*Don't be afraid,*" I hear her say.

Then I am startled by a sound of laughter coming from the living room. Who is here? My heart races. I get up. Alex wakes up and sees me. "What is it?"

"I don't know I heard my angel say not to be afraid. I thought I heard laughter coming from the living room. Is someone in the house?"

Oddly a calmness comes over me. I turn the light on get up and so does Alex. We walk slowly to the doorway and see, by the light of the fire, a sight like none other, an unbelievable sight. Maurice and the dogs come walking next to us.

There by the fire's bright light, sitting in Alex's big red chair, is volunteer Jerome Golightly, dressed as he was this morning in his Santa suit. He's with Winter, who is sitting happily on his lap. He's whispering something to her then he laughs his Santa laugh.

I'm speechless, frozen like a statue. He looks up.

"Ah it is such Merry Christmas dear ones, isn't it? I don't mean to frighten you." For a moment I'm alarmed but it's Jerome, Santa to all the kids today. How did he know where we live? What is happening? My angel said not to be afraid.

Jerome remains seated petting Winter who closes her eyes. "Don't be afraid. You see Gayle and Alex, I wanted to check on Winter and see Buddy. But you need to know something." The other dogs are wagging their tails and trot to Jerome. He bends down to give them a pet. Alex tries to speak but can't.

"I want you to know how pleased I am with you both, how kind and generous you were with your time and abilities to help the animals. God bless you. But I came to hug Winter and Buddy tonight and tell Winter a few things before I go." He stands placing Winter ever so gently on the rug.

"Jerome," says Alex. "You're welcome here, but how did you get in our house? Please what is going on?"

"No need to be alarmed. I know you'll keep our secret safe. You see, I'm really one of them, an angel. You know, Alex, like your mother Rachel, like Ken. I live life among the humans. I found Winter alone, early one morning, looking forlorn. Heaven told me her gentleman had gone but she didn't know where. I picked her up and flew her to Mystic Bay, above your house telling her you would be taking her home from the shelter. She would be warm and safe with you and go on a quest with you to save the dog, Buddy. Vince had found Buddy and then lost him that day when Burt picked him up, trying to save the poor dog. But what I didn't know was how many other animals you would save and how some adults would find happiness in their lives again too.

"We angels can only guide, not fix everything. I think you understand by now. You have the abilities like your mother to find the lost ones, the broken-hearted ones. You too, Alex, have the gift, such a loving gift, the gift of intuition."

Alex says, "Are you taking Winter with you? Gayle has been wondering if she's really a dog angel."

I still can't talk as Angel Jerome shakes his head no as he pets Winter's head. "I told Winter that day to wait for me. She understood that one night, I would come to see her and her new home and her family and Buddy. Tonight, she asked me if she could stay. I guess I needed to tell her when I flew her over your house that this house was her forever home. I didn't tell her then that her gentleman companion has gone to heaven's realm and is waiting for her someday, but not now. She's been waiting for me by the fireplace. I realized today when I saw you that your heart was filled with worry and that I indeed needed to come see her, and show you myself as I really am. I have assured her she is yours and you are hers."

He pets all the dogs one by one. "Good Winter, Buddy, Ralph, Magic. And Maurice, you're one of my favorites."

Alex asks, "How do you know all the animals' names?"

We angels know every one of their names, lucky for us. You see dogs and cats are all special angels." He turns his back to us and walks out the patio door into the starry night. "A fine night for flying."

Jerome is an angel?

Finally, I manage to speak. "Thank you, Jerome."

"You are most welcome and Merry Christmas. Winter is not only the dog who came for Christmas. She's the dog who came to stay."

In the crisp air we follow him. At the edge of the patio, he faces west, looking up to the glimmering stars. His gossamer wings form magically from his shoulders. They are magnificent glowing gold and silver streams of light, like starlight and moonshine. He turns and winks at us as if he is the real Santa. "I'll be seeing you." With a nod he takes flight above our house and trees then over Aunt Nancy and Uncle Dick's house too. Angel Jerome turns and waves flying on toward the harbor into the night until he's gone from our sight. The only sound is the sound of the sea.

We see Jamie Bond by the streetlight on the side of the house, walking down the street with Bondo as he does around midnight each night. Tonight, he is walking two dogs, Bondo with Riley for her first midnight walk.

Jamie sees us and waves. Bondo is looking up. Riley too. We know all dogs and cats can see angels.

Can they still see Angel Jerome flying away? But then all the animals look up to the east in synchronicity. Alex and I turn our attention to where they're looking. We see Ken's little owl above us and angel dust whisps flying towards us. We both can see him as the animals have. It's Angel Ken flying above. The angel dust encircles us for a moment then disappears, falling to the ground like ethereal snowflakes melting around us. We wave but does he see us?

"Ken's flying on to catch up with his little owl or maybe just maybe he'll see Angel Jerome along the way," I say to Alex.

"How many angels really do live as humans around us, thousands or millions?"

"We're not meant to know, I guess. All I know, my husband, is that I'm glad you are part angel."

Alex smiles and says, "We've witnessed a Christmas miracle tonight!"

We stare still at the night sky yawning at the same time. We turn and walk into the house. Alex says, "Time to really go to bed now, guys. We've seen two angels tonight. How about that?"

We both bend down to hug Winter as she goes to her bed by the fireplace. The low embers shine light in her eyes. "Alex, she's happy I can tell."

Alex tells her, "Sleep happy Winter and dream of your Angel Jerome.

We walk into our bedroom. The soft light from the kitchen will keep her company as always. We cover each dog and Maurice with a little blanket. Buddy is cozy in his new bed. He looks toward the door as if he's wondering if Winter will come in too. "Goodnight Buddy, we love you, forever." His eyes close and I know he already senses this is where he belongs. We turn the lights out, falling into the bed. "Do you think Winter will wait for Jerome each night?"

"I don't get that feeling now but her love for him is special. To think he flew her over our house early the morning before you met her. He'll be back someday." He laughs, "But will he wear his Santa suit?"

"I hope so." I smile thinking of Jerome, a jolly old angel, a Christmas angel.

Nestling down in the covers, I can tell Alex is almost at sleep's door. He always falls asleep so fast. I lie awake for a time each night.

The covers are warm. I look toward the bedroom door and I have to blink, joyously. Winter is walking into our room. The nightlight reflects in her eyes. Is she really going to sleep in her bed next to ours and Buddy's? It's been waiting for her. She comes close to my side of the bed and I look into her dreamy eyes. I can see the past. Her companion, the older man's spirit is smiling beside her. Then my ability to see the past is gone, a captured moment in time. Winter nestles into her bed. She's lying next to sleeping Buddy. At last.

In the dark of night, I catch a glimpse of the stars shining outside our window. Somewhere out there, Angels Ken and Jerome are doing God's work as they fly in the wee hours of the late December morning. The soft breathing of the dearest animals lulls me now. I place my hand in Alex's hand. I see Dukie's happy spirit in my mind and hear my Angel whisper, *"Sweet dreams."*

Chapter 20

Acknowledgements

T hankfulness fills my heart for the following brilliant people. Don Mc-Cauley, my publicist, is an extraordinary publicist, always encouraging me and he works tirelessly to get my books out into the world and market place.

My talented editor, Barbara Youngs, has given me her expertise with thorough editing, enhancing my books to their fullest potential.

The storyline has parts taken from true experiences of my husband, Dave's and mine when rescuing dogs and cats. Also, my forever friend, Maggie has encountered angels. She dreamed of her dear departed dog, Cera. In the dream, Cera showed her a dog at a rescue who would run to her and Maggie would adopt her. That dream came true. Amber the fluffy white dog in her dream, ran to her just as Cera showed Maggie. Amber is gone now to heaven, but I wrote her in the book as a character as many of our friend's dogs are featured.

To my children, Mike and Liz, I appreciate your love and support of all my work, all written in memory of their dear sister, my late daughter, Kate. We lost her many years ago, but by imagining and creating the town of Mystic Bay books where angels live as humans, has given me much joy and comfort.

To my dear husband, Dave, I give thanks for his ongoing love and encouragement for my writing, listening to paragraphs as I write for many years, even giving me suggestions for scenarios. He and I are both advocates of rescuing animals and have rescued many together.

I thank and send love to all my friends and their animals that make appearances in my novels. I send love to all the animals I have been honored to live with in the past, present and future.

Finally, I thank the angel I met appearing as a man to me years ago as I traveled after Kate passed away. My dear friend, Nancy, knew I needed a respite. She took me to Houston for a girl's trip where we encountered the man's presence. It was a surreal happenchance we thought meeting him two days in a row in different Texas towns. His comforting words changed my grief's path. The miracles angels bring us make me believe in angels and Love's triumph.

sharpejody76@gmail.com